THE QUEEN'S
BABY SCANDAL

THE QUEEN'S BABY SCANDAL

MAISEY YATES

MILLS & BOON

First published in Great Britain 2019
by Mills & Boon, an imprint of HarperCollins*Publishers*
1 London Bridge Street, London, SE1 9GF

Large Print edition 2020

© 2019 Maisey Yates

ISBN: 978-0-263-08434-4

Printed and bound in Great Britain
by CPI Group (UK) Ltd, Croydon, CR0 4YY

To Jackie, Megan, Nicole and Rusty.

Finding true friends who understand you, relate to you, make you laugh and even try to politely respond to the 100 raccoon pictures you send them a day is a rare thing. I think it might even be magic.

Thank you for being my friends.

CHAPTER ONE

QUEEN ASTRID VON BJORNLAND had never been to a club before. But she was reasonably familiar with the layout of the Ice Palace, nestled in the Italian Alps, hidden away from commoners and social riffraff—as defined by Mauro Bianchi, the billionaire owner of the establishment—in spite of the fact that it was a place she'd never before visited.

She and Latika had done an intense amount of research on the subject prior to hatching their plan, and image searches of the facility itself had been involved. Though, the findings had been sparse.

Mauro was intensely protective of the image of the club as exclusive. And the only photographs that existed were photographs that had been officially sanctioned by Mauro himself, and included only the main areas, and none of the VIP locations that the many articles Astrid had read stated were stationed throughout the club.

Her palms were sweaty, but she knew that the invitation that she held in her hand was good enough.

Latika had assured her of that. And Latika was never wrong.

When Astrid had been looking to hire an assistant the year before her father had passed, she'd made discreet inquiries among the circle of dignitaries and royalty she knew, and Latika had appeared the next day. Polished, sleek and just a bit too good to be true.

It hadn't taken long for Astrid to realize Latika was hiding something.

"I had to get away from my father. He's a very rich man, and looking to consolidate that wealth by marrying me off to a man who is... He's not a good man. I will need to stay out of the spotlight completely. So all of my work will be done quietly, efficiently and with me out of the picture."

That was all Astrid had needed to hear. She knew all about the looming specter of poten-

tial arranged marriages and overly control-
ling fathers.

And so, she had hired Latika on the spot.

She was a whiz of an assistant—and had become an even better friend, and ally—and able
to conjure up near magic with the snap of her
fingers. In this case, magic had included: an
excuse for Astrid to go to Italy, a car rented
on the sly, an extravagant and extravagantly
skimpy designer dress, jewels and shoes, and
a near impossible invitation to the party.

And now Astrid was standing and waiting
behind the thick velvet rope, in line, for entry.

Astrid had never waited in a line before. Not
once in her life.

Astrid had never waited full stop.

She had been born five minutes before her
twin brother, Prince Gunnar, much to the dis-
may of her father and the entire house of no-
bility. And that had essentially set the tone for
her entire life.

A tone that had led to this particular plan, as
dangerous, unlikely and foolhardy as it was.

All of those adjectives had belonged to Latika. Who had scolded Astrid the entire time she had aided her in putting the plan together.

Latika had *many* opinions, but none of them really mattered. Both in terms of what she would help Astrid accomplish, and in terms of what Astrid would choose to do. She would make happen whatever Astrid asked her to make happen. And that was the simple truth of it.

Astrid tugged at the hem of her impossibly short white dress. It was daring, and nothing like she would wear in her real life, but that had been part of the plan.

She could not look like Queen Astrid. If her brother found out, he would come down to the club and physically drag her out. Not to mention if any of the various government officials found out, they would do the same.

But she was doing what had to be done to wrest control of her kingdom into her own hands. Control of her future.

She would find other ways if need be, but this plan had come together with so much expert timing that Astrid was willing to chance it for several reasons.

And, she had been willing to wear a gown that was essentially a suit jacket with nothing beneath it. The neckline gaped, showing curves and angles of her body she normally kept well hidden.

Her red hair was loose, cascading over her shoulders, and she was wearing a single, long emerald on a chain, which swayed perilously between her cleavage and made her feel like she was drawing attention.

Of course, if she wasn't drawing attention to her cleavage, then she was calling attention to her legs, with that abbreviated hemline in the sky-high heels. And perhaps her rear, where she knew the white dress clung with a kind of saucy cheekiness. At least, that was what Latika had told her.

But the final thing that Latika had said to her as she had dropped her in front of the queue for the club was that she absolutely had to be back out at the curb by two in the morning.

The timing was essential, and if she missed the timing at all, not only could the plan be in jeopardy, but Latika's job *certainly* would be. And by extension possibly Latika herself, given that her position at the palace had been insulation for her for the past three years.

Astrid was the figurehead for her country. And she had power, it was true. But her father's antiquated board, along with the elected government, had authority and if something was ever put to a vote, whether it be a member of staff or law, then Astrid would be outweighed. It would be thus, she had been assured, even if Gunnar had been made king. Even if he were not born five minutes *after* his sister.

Though, Astrid was not convinced of this.

And she had found a loophole. And that loophole was why she was here.

It certainly had nothing to do with Mauro Bianchi. Not in the personal sense. She didn't even know the man, after all. But she knew about him. Everyone did. A self-made billionaire who had risen up from abject poverty thanks to his grit and determination.

In Astrid's opinion, had this been the Middle Ages, he would have been a marauding conqueror. And as she was dealing with arcane laws more firmly in the Middle Ages than in the modern era, that had only made him all the more attractive to her as she set about hatching her plan.

She took a step forward in line as all of the people shuffled upward, and she found herself facing a large, grim-looking bouncer with a pronounced scar running across the length of his face.

She squared her shoulders, and then, changed tactics. She arched her breasts outward instead, and rather than affecting her typical severe glance, she went with a pout, just as she and Latika had been practicing in her hotel room tonight before they had gone out.

"Here is my invitation," she said, somehow feeling like she hadn't quite gotten down the simper that the other women in the line had thrown out when they had presented their invitations to the bouncer.

But it didn't matter. The invitation—while for a person who didn't exist—was for the person she was playing, and it was legitimate.

"Of course," he said, looking her over, something he did in his gaze that Astrid had never had directed at her before. "Enjoy the party, Ms. Steele."

He kept the card firmly in his hand, and ushered her inside.

It was a strange and wondrous place, some rooms carved entirely of ice, and requiring coats for entry, others fashioned of steel and glittering lights, everything fading into each other like a twisting, glittering paradise.

Astrid had grown up surrounded by luxury. But it was not a modern luxury. Not in the least. It was velvet and drapes, gold and ornate wrought iron. Cold marble and granite.

This was color, twisted metal and light. Fire and ice all melded together in an escape for the senses that verged on decadent.

There was a dance floor that was suspended up above a carved icy chamber. It glittered and twisted, casting refracted light all around. Railings around the outside of the platform prevented the revelers from falling below. She had never seen anything quite like it.

It was like something from a dream. Or a fairy tale.

If fairy tales contained house music.

And for the first time, a slight thrill went through her.

She had come about this entire plan with the grimness of a general going to war.

At least, that was what she had told herself. She had told herself that it had nothing to do with the fact that she wanted one night of freedom.

Had told herself that Mauro Bianchi had not been her target because he was attractive. Because he had a reputation for showing women the kinds of pleasure that was normally found only in books. No.

She had told herself that he was a *strategic* target.

A man with no royal connection or blood, which would make the claiming of her position even more unquestionable. Had told herself that a known playboy was sensible because as an unpracticed seductress, she would need a target that would have very low resistance.

Because she knew where to find him.

She had told herself all of those things, and the more she had read articles about him, the more she had seen images of him, his face, his body, the dark tattoos that covered his skin...

She had told herself that none of that mattered. That his beauty was secondary, and indeed only a perk in that it was a genetic point of desirability.

But now that she was here… Now that she was here in this club with dance music wrapping itself around her skin, and the thrill of her deceit rocketing through her like adrenaline, a smile spread across her lips.

Freedom.

This was a moment of freedom. A moment to last a lifetime.

Yes, she was doing this to claim the maximum amount of freedom a woman in her position ever could. But even so, she would go back to her life of service when all this was said and done. But this… This was a moment out of time.

Not a moment to think about the future. Of what it would be like to finally have the power over her country she deserved. To finally get out of her father's stranglehold. Not a moment to ponder how the ache of loneliness she felt inside might finally be assuaged by holding a child of her own. A child she would love no matter what.

She was Alice, through a looking glass. Not Astrid.

And she was going to seduce a man for the first time in her life. Possibly the last.

All she had to do was find him. And then she saw him, there could be no mistaking him. He was up on a platform above the dance floor, surveying the party below. It could be only him. That dark, enigmatic gaze rolling over the crowd with an air of unquestionable authority.

Astrid was royalty in Bjornland. She was the queen.

But there was no mistaking that here in this club, Mauro Bianchi was king.

The king of sin, of vice, of pleasure.

The kind of king who would never be welcome in a state and steady nation such as hers. But the perfect king for tonight.

She took a breath and made her way over to the stairs, thanking a lifetime of deportment for her ability to climb them with ease even in those spiked, crystal heels she had on her feet. She let her fingers drift along the rail in a seductive manner, the kind that she had been warned against as a girl. She had been taught to convey herself as cool. Sexless, really.

She was the first female monarch in Bjorn-land since the 1500s. The weight of the crown for her could never have been anything but heavy.

Her father had ever been resentful of the fact that it was the daughter who had been born first. Resentful. Distrustful. Doubtful.

But her mother… It was her mother who had made absolutely certain that there would be no creative shifting of birth orders.

Astrid had been born first. And her mother had had the announcement issued with speed and finality.

Her mother had also made sure that Astrid's education had been complete. That she had been trained in the art of war. Not just the kind found on the battlefield, but the kind she would face in any and all political arenas.

There was a ruthlessness, her mother had told her, to all rulers. And a queen would need to hone her ruthlessness to a razor-sharp point, and wield it with more exacting brutality than any king.

And so she had been instructed on how to hold herself, how to be beautiful, without being sexual.

She was throwing all of it away right in that moment. Allowing her hips to sway, allowing her fingertips to caress the railing like she might a lover.

She had never had a lover.

But it was the aim of tonight.

And so, she could forget everything she had learned, or rather, could turn it upside down in this place that was like a mirror of her normal life.

That was how she felt. As if she'd stepped through the looking glass. As if she was on the other side of wealth and beauty. Not the weighted, austere version, but this frivolous palace made of ice. Transient and decadent. For no purpose other than pleasure.

She tossed her hair over her shoulder, and the moment she stepped onto the dance floor, she looked up.

Her eyes collided with his.

He saw her. He more than saw her.

It was as if there was an electric current in the air.

And so she did something she would have never done on any other day when her eyes connected with a strange man's from across the room.

She licked her lips. Slowly. Deliberately.

And then she smiled.

She tossed her hair over her shoulder and continued onto the dance floor.

There were many women, and men, dancing by themselves and so she threw herself into the middle of them, and she allowed the rhythm to guide her movements.

She knew the steps to any number of formal dances. Music composed to complement a dance, not music created to lead it.

But she let the beat determine the shift of her hips, the arch in her spine. And for one, wonderful moment she felt like she was simply part of the crowd. Exhilarating. Freeing.

And then she felt the crowd move. But it was more than that. There was a change in the air. In everything around her.

And she knew already what it meant.

The king was on the dance floor.

She turned, and she nearly ran into a broad chest, her face coming just to his collarbone.

He was wearing a black jacket, black shirt with the top two buttons undone, exposing a wedge of skin and dark hair, tantalizing and forbidden—in her estimation—as no dignitary she had ever encountered would approach her without his tie done up tight.

She looked up, and her heart nearly stopped. And then when a smile tipped his lips upward, it accelerated again.

Photographs had not prepared her.

She'd first seen him in a gossip magazine a year ago when Astrid had brought in a copy of a particularly vile rag that had featured a scandal about Astrid's brother—who had not spent life on his best behavior in the slightest.

But it wasn't Gunnar and his naked exploits with a French model that had held Astrid's attention. First of all, it was a terribly *common* thing. Even for Gunnar. It wasn't even interesting.

But second of all…

Oh, there had been Mauro. A dissolute, salacious, scandalous playboy in a tux, with one woman clinging to each arm as he walked through one of his clubs.

Her heart had stopped. The world had stopped.

That was just a photograph.

In person…

He was beautiful, but not in the way the word was typically used. He was far too masculine a thing for simple beauty. Hard and angular like a rock, his jaw square and sculpted, his lips perfectly shaped and firm looking. His dark eyes were like chips of obsidian, the lights on the dance floor swallowed up in those fathomless depths.

He said nothing, and she wouldn't have been able to hear him anyway. But he extended his hand, and she took his, the spark of fire that ignited at that point of contact spreading over her body like a ripple in the water. Sharp and shocking at its core, rolling over her wider and broader as it expanded.

He caught her and held her against his body.

She had danced with men before, but they had not held her like this. So close that her breasts were crushed to hard, muscular midsections, a large commanding hand low on her back.

And then his lips touched her ear, his whisper husky. "I've never seen you before."

She moved back, tipping her chin upward so that she could see him, so that she could look him full in the face. Except, she could hardly sustain it. She looked down.

And he captured her chin, forcing her to meet his gaze again. If she hadn't been wearing those heels she would have been so incredibly dwarfed by him there would have been no responding. But he lowered his head, and she leaned in.

"Because I've never been here before."

"It's always nice to see an unfamiliar face," he said, this time brushing her hair back from her face as he whispered.

"Dance with me," she said, not bothering to whisper this time.

The way that the rather predatory grin slid over his mouth told her that he understood.

That she wanted to do more than dance.

His eyes burned into hers as he gripped her hips, dragging her toward him as they moved in time with the music. She felt his touch everywhere, not just where he had his hands, but all the points in between, down deep, in the most intimate parts of her. She had danced with men before, but it had never been like this. Of course, the perfectly polished aristocrats who had always attended the balls she'd been at had never been anything like this.

There was an element of danger to this man. And she found herself drawn to it.

In fact, she found she wanted to fling herself against it. Against him. She had always been asked to be strong, but she had also been sheltered in many ways. Her take on the world was theoretical. And now, she was being tasked with ruling an entire country, while still suffering from that same fate.

Power, but with chains around it.

She wanted to test herself. To test those bonds.

It was what she was here to do.

"Maybe you could show me your club."

His grip tightened on her, and he looked at her for a long moment, before taking her hand and leading her from the dance floor. He held on to her as he took her down the stairs, away from the pulsing music. But they didn't go back to the entry, where people had crowded in. Instead, he moved her down a slim corridor with black flooring that had gold light shooting through the spaces in the tile. He pushed open a door that simply looked like another obsidian panel. "You will want a coat," he said, not taking one for himself, but offering her a snow-white one from a rack by the door.

"Thank you," she said, taking the coat from him and putting it on.

She quite wondered if covering her body might put her out of this advantage, but he was the one leading her, so she supposed she had better follow instruction.

Another thing she had never been very good at. But unlike waiting, it was something she had been asked to do quite a bit.

Something she now wished to avoid.

The room he led her into was made entirely of ice, the walls carved in intricate designs, crystalline, nearly see-through. By a deep navy blue couch was a wall that allowed a mirror view, however rippling and obscured, of revelers next door.

"You are quite bold," he said. "Asking me to show you my club."

"And yet, you seem to be showing me."

"I don't know that you realize just how rare it is for me to take a woman up on such an offer."

"And here I thought you took women up on such offers on a nightly basis. I've read about you."

His lips twisted upward in a cynical impersonation of a smile. "Of course you have."

"I'm sorry," she said. "Should I pretend I don't know who you are? Should I pretend that this is simply a chance encounter, and I came to your club with no prior knowledge of who you were?"

He affected a casual shrug. "Many women would."

"Perhaps those women have the luxury of time. I don't."

"You don't have a bomb strapped to your chest, do you?"

She swallowed hard, letting the edges of her

coat fall open, revealing the only thing she had against her chest, that emerald, which immediately felt cold in the icy room. "You're welcome to look for yourself."

His gaze flickered over her body, and it didn't stay cool. "I see. Someone waiting for you at home, then?"

That was close enough to the truth. "Yes," she said.

"Can I have your name?"

"Alice," she said.

"Alice," he repeated. "From?"

She knew her English was quite good, but that it would also be colored by an accent. His was too, though different from hers. She liked the way it sounded. She wanted to hear his voice speak his native tongue. And hers. What sort of accent would it give to her own language? And what sorts of words might he say…?

"England," she said. "Not originally. But for most of my life."

"What brings you to Italy?"

"Your party," she said.

"I see. Are you an enthusiast when it comes to clubs, or are you a sex tourist?"

The words were bold, and she knew that she was playing a bold game and she needed to be able to return in kind.

"In this instance, I suppose it's sex tourism."

"Am I to understand that you saw my picture in the news and decided to make a trip all the way to my club for sex?"

Nothing he'd said was a lie. There might be more in her reasoning, but she had seen his photo. And she had wanted him on sight.

"Chemistry is a fairly powerful thing."

"Can you feel chemistry with a photograph?"

"I didn't even have to go looking for you," she said. "You came to me. So that makes me wonder if it's possible."

And that was the honest truth.

She had never expected Mauro Bianchi to approach her. No, she had expected that she would have to chase him down. That she would be the one pursuing him. And yet, he had simply appeared. And now, he had taken her to a VIP room. So it all rather did beg the question if chemistry could be that obvious.

The expression on his hard face did something then, and she couldn't quite put into words what that was. He looked quite irritated, but at the same time perhaps a bit impressed with her boldness and her reasoning. And he couldn't argue. Because here they were, sitting in this private suite, strangers who had never met until only a moment ago.

"I think the only thing to do then is perhaps test your theory," he said, his voice lowering to a silky purr.

"That is what I'm here for," she said, fighting to keep her voice smooth.

"Perhaps you would like to see my private suite."

"I would like that very much," she said.

This was moving much quicker than she had anticipated. But it was also going exactly according to plan.

She had expected…obstacles. Resistance.

Perhaps because the last year of her life had been marked by such things. Endless resistance from her father's officials. Endless proclamations being made. Demands that she be married. The concern over her producing an heir, as for her, there would be a time limit, unlike with men.

But they had not counted on one thing. Because they had not educated themselves, not to the extent that she had.

Men. With their arrogance. Their certainty that they were right. That they could not be bested, least of all by her.

She had read the laws. She had studied. She had made sure, above all else, that she was prepared for her position, and that she would not be taken by surprise.

Because for the protection of the queen, for the protection of the throne, if she claimed that her issue had no father, that it was the queen's alone.

And there were no questions of legitimacy. A law set into motion to protect the queen from marauders, Vikings and barbarians, anyone who might seek to use her to claim power.

And at this point in history, in time, used to protect the queen from forced marriages, and politicians who overexerted their power, and sought to keep a nation in the dark ages.

All she needed was her marauder.

And she had found him.

"Yes," she said. "Let's go to your room."

CHAPTER TWO

BY THE TIME they had gone through a maze of high-gloss marble corridors and arrived at Mauro's suite, Astrid was trembling. She did her best to try to disguise it, and hope that he would perhaps assume it was because they were surrounded by ice. But the fact of the matter was, the pieces of the structure that were not made of ice were quite comfortable, and she imagined he assumed no such thing.

She was so good at pretending to be confident, serene and as if she were in possession of every secret in all the world, that sometimes she even convinced herself such things were true.

Sometimes she forgot what she really was.

She was a queen, that much was true. A queen with quite a lot of power, education and confidence that was rightly earned.

She was also a woman who had been kept separate from peers for most of her life while she focused on her education. A woman who had danced with a man, but never, ever kissed one.

She was a virgin queen, above reproach as her mother had always instructed her to be.

But matters had become desperate, and so had she.

And she was waging war in a sense, and that meant she could not afford nerves. Even as they rolled over her in a wave, the reality of the utter disparity between the two of them a strange and intense sort of drug.

An aphrodisiac and a bit of a terror.

She was used to having a mantle of power over her, but he didn't know who she was. And here, in this private room he had just ushered her into, he was the experienced one. He was physically so much more powerful than she could ever hope to be, and her guards were well and truly dismissed. She had no one to snap her fingers for and call for rescue. She didn't even have her phone, as she and Latika had agreed that her being traceable to the club in any manner wasn't acceptable.

It was why the timing of everything was so crucial.

His suite was warm, wonderfully appointed with furs in a dark ebony, and bright white cotton spread over a massive mattress.

She looked over at him, and his lips curved as he closed the door behind them.

"Second thoughts?"

"No," she said, squaring her shoulders. "Not at all."

"I did not take a woman who would freely admit to being a sex tourist as one who would be overcome by the nerves of an innocent."

She laughed, so very grateful for all the years she had spent at various political events dodging barbs of every sort, allowing her an easy smile and confident stare even while verbal daggers were being thrown her way. "Naturally not. It's only that… We haven't even kissed yet. And I do want a bit of certainty regarding chemistry."

"A woman of high standards."

"Exceptionally," she said. "I should have

mentioned to you that I am—as far as sex tourists go—not a backpacker. I only go first-class. And if things are not to my liking, I don't stay."

A dark flame burned yet higher in his eyes, a clear response to what he obviously took as a challenge.

"I was going to offer you a drink," he said.

"Why? Because you think you should fare better if my senses are dulled?"

He chuckled and moved to her, wrapping his arm around her waist and pulling her against his body. He took hold of her chin, keeping her face steady as he stared down into her eyes.

"Let us test the chemistry, then," he said, his voice rough.

He bent down, closing the distance between them, and it was like a flame had ignited across her skin.

His kiss was rough, commanding and intense in ways she had not imagined a kiss could ever be. And this was why she had chosen him. It was why he was the only one she could fathom being with.

She had known, somehow, that he would be

the one who could make her forget, for just a moment, what she was. That he could be the one who made her exult in feeling delicate. Fragile.

His masculinity was so rough. So exciting. His kiss that of a conqueror. And how she reveled in it. Gloried in his touch. His hands, large and impossibly rough, held her face steady as he angled his head and took the kiss deeper, deeper still, his tongue invading her, making her tremble, making her knees weak.

When they parted, he stared down at her, those eyes shot through with intensity. "Is that quite enough chemistry for you?" he asked.

"Yes," she whispered. "I think that is exactly the chemistry I was looking for."

He stood back and shrugged his jacket off, tossing it carelessly toward the couch on the opposite side of the room, and then he began to unbutton his shirt.

Astrid's mouth went dry as she watched him expose his body. His chest was hard looking and muscular, his abs clearly defined, with just the right amount of dark hair dusted over those sculpted ridges. And he had tattoos.

Dark, swirling ink that covered his shoulder, part of his chest geometric patterns that she couldn't quite divine the meaning of.

But the beauty of tonight was that it didn't matter.

It didn't matter what any of this meant to him. All that mattered was what it meant to her.

Freedom. Wildness.

A night with her very own barbarian.

The kind of man she would scarcely have been allowed to speak to if her handlers were present. Much less be alone in a room with.

Much less be on the verge of…

"Pictures don't do you justice," she said.

"I have a feeling that dress doesn't do *you* justice," he returned. "But I would like to see for a fact if this is true."

With shaking fingers, she reached around behind her back and slowly lowered the zip to her dress, letting the soft white fabric release itself from her body and fall to the ground, a pale, silken pool at her feet.

She was still wearing those impossibly high

heels and a pair of white panties. Nothing more. He seemed to approve.

Her breasts grew heavy, her nipples tight, her body overcome with restless anticipation.

Then he sprung into action, his muscles all languid grace and lethal precision as he took her in his arms and swept her up off the floor, carrying her over to that large bed and setting her down on the soft, black fur that was spread over the top.

He said something in Italian, something completely unfamiliar to her, something she assumed was something like a curse, or just something so filthy no one would have ever seen fit to teach her. Anticipation shimmered deep and low inside her.

He drew away from the bed, his eyes never leaving hers as he slowly undid his belt, drawing the zipper on his pants down as he divested himself of the rest of his clothing, leaving him completely naked in front of her.

Astrid was one for research. For being prepared when going to war. And as such, she had done a fair share of figuring out just what happened between men and women in bed, not simply in the perfunctory sense. She had done a bit of pictorial research.

But it had not prepared her for this. For him. All of him.

He was quite a bit more of a man than she had ever seen, and she had certainly never been in the same room as a naked man before. So deliciously, impossibly male.

"You are stunning," he said, advancing on her, moving toward the bed. Her stomach twisted, fear and excitement twining together and becoming something so exciting, so unbearably potent she could scarcely breathe, let alone think. She licked her lips, grabbing hold of the waistband of her panties and pushing them down her legs as she arched her bottom up off the mattress, managing to pull them only down to her knees, then uncertain how to continue. He clearly took her uncertainty as an intentional coquettishness, and she was happy to have him think so. He growled, moving down to the bed and grabbing hold of the scrap of lace and wrenching it from her body. Leaving her bare and exposed to him.

His eyes roamed over her hungrily, and there

was something so incredibly close and raw about the moment that Astrid had to close her eyes.

Because there was no title here to protect her. No designer clothing, no guards. Nothing between her and this man. This man who seemed to want her, though he'd had many other women.

Astrid was used to being special. Singular. But she had none of the hallmarks here that made her any of that. She was simply a woman. She was not a queen.

And yet.

And yet he still wanted her.

She began to push the shoes off she was wearing, and he moved over her, gripping her wrists and drawing them up over her head. "Leave them," he said, pressing a kiss to her mouth before skimming his hand over her curves, his thumb moving over her nipple, an arrow of pleasure hitting her down low, making her feel aching and hollow. And then he kissed her neck, her collarbone, down to the plump curve of her breast, his tongue tracing a line around the tightened bud there.

She squirmed, arching against him, but he held her wrists fast with one hand while he continued his exploration with his mouth, and his other hand, which had moved to her hip, and was now drifting between her thighs.

Her hips bowed up off the bed when he touched her there. His fingers delving expertly into her silken folds, finding her embarrassingly wet for him.

But then, there was no point to embarrassment. Not now. Not with him.

This was her one night of freedom.

Her one night to claim a lifetime of greater freedom.

And she would not do it with a whimper. But with a roar.

She moved her hips sinuously, in time with his strokes, with the soft suction of his mouth on her breast.

He moved his thumb over the most sensitive place between her legs, stroking back and forth, and she cried out, caught off guard by the intensity of the sensations he created there. When her release broke over her, it was a shock, shattering her like a fragile glass pane, the sharp, jagged edges of her pleasure making her feel weak and vulnerable.

She clung to his shoulders, kissing his mouth, moving her hands over his finely muscled back as she did. She shifted beneath him, feeling the hard, heavy weight of his erection against her thigh. He began to move away.

"It's okay," she said in a rush, while she still had her wits about her.

And she knew what he would interpret it to mean.

She also knew, from much of her reading, that he was a very careful man when it came to these matters.

But she was counting on him being lost in the moment. She was counting on him being mortal.

This was her killing blow, so to speak, and she had to deliver it and not falter.

"Please," she whispered against his mouth and she rolled her hips upward, so that his erection was settled against her wet heat, and she arched back and forth, the pleasure making her see stars.

She could see, mirrored in his own eyes, no

small amount of that same pleasure. Of that desire. That need. He was no stronger than she, and she had been counting on that.

He growled, wrapping his hand around his arousal and positioning himself firmly against her before he slammed inside.

His savage kiss swallowed her cry of pain, and she knew that he misinterpreted it as pleasure as he lost control and pulled out slowly before thrusting back home again.

Astrid closed her eyes tight, willing herself to make it through this without crying, without embarrassing herself.

She simply hadn't anticipated it would hurt quite so badly.

He was lost to it, and she needed him to be. She only wished that she could join him.

She held his shoulders, burying her face in his neck.

And then he seemed to grasp some kind of hold on himself, his movement slowing, his pelvis rocking forward, hitting her just so, and creating a spark inside her she had been convinced would be lost in this encounter.

But it wasn't. Oh, it wasn't.

Suddenly she felt it. Deep and pleasurable and building inside her. Overcoming the pain. Overcoming everything else. It was wonderful. Beautiful and real.

He kissed her as he held her hips and drove home, hard and relentless, and welcome now. It was like she couldn't get enough. As if he couldn't go deep enough, hard enough.

There was something mystical in this joining that she couldn't figure out, but it had something to do with that instant spark that had happened when they laid eyes on each other.

Maybe even with the spark she felt when she had first seen his picture.

And when her release broke over her, it was different from before. Her body gripped his, drawing him deeper, pulsing around him as light exploded behind her eyes. And she didn't feel shattered. She felt renewed. Reinforced as he broke apart, as he trembled in her arms, this large, muscular, experienced man, reduced to shaking as he spent himself inside her.

They lay there, not for long. Only a few moments. While Astrid tried to catch her breath.

And then she heard the sound of a clock strike two chimes.

"What time is it?"

"Two?" he asked, his words muffled, sleepy.

"I have to go," she said. She scrambled out of bed in a panic, hunting around for clothing, getting dressed as quickly as possible while Mauro looked on.

"You're not going to just leave."

"I have to," she said, desperation clawing at her.

"Give me your name."

"Alice," she said.

"Your full name. I wish to find you again."

"Alice Steele," she said, the lie tripping off her tongue.

"That's wrong," he said.

"No," she said, panic like a wild thing inside her. "It's on the invitation."

"That isn't your name," he said, his dark eyes seeing straight into her.

She straightened and looked at him for one last, lingering moment, before she fled. She made her way down the halls, thankful that he was naked, and therefore wouldn't be able to move as quickly as she.

By the time she made it out to the main part of the club, Mauro was right behind her. She kept on running, one of her shoes flying off as she did, as she made an uneven escape down the stairs and tumbled straight into the limo that Latika was driving.

"Go," she said.

"Were you successful?"

She looked back at the doorway and saw him standing there, holding her shoe in his hand.

"Just go," she said, panic and emotion rising up in her throat.

And Queen Astrid escaped into the night, without her virginity, but very hopefully, carrying her heir.

CHAPTER THREE

"FORGIVE ME FOR saying so, sir, but you do not seem yourself."

Mauro Bianchi, dissolute playboy and renowned billionaire, looked over at his assistant Carlo, and treated him to a fearsome scowl. "You are *not* forgiven."

Not because his assistant was not wrong in his observation. No. Mauro was not himself, and had not been for the past three months. He could not pretend he didn't know why. He did.

He was held utterly captive by memories of a bewitching redhead, and a stolen hour in his private suite of rooms.

By the way she had run from him, leaving him holding her shoe.

And by the discovery he'd made when he had gone back to his bedroom.

The blood left on the sheets.

It was entirely possible the woman had started her period, he supposed.

Also… Also a possibility that she had been a virgin. Though he could not fathom a virgin speaking as boldly as she had.

A virgin going back to a man's room for sex, and only sex.

And she had said there was someone waiting for her at home.

He was captivated by the mystery of her, by the erotic memory of her, and nothing he did allowed him to shake it.

Apparently his staff was beginning to notice.

Certainly, the paparazzi had.

Wondering why he'd yet to turn up anywhere with a new woman on his arm, and there was endless speculation about that.

Some even suggesting that he might be in a real relationship, rather than just engaging in one of his usual transient sexual dalliances.

Of course, the press could not be more wrong.

His bed was cold and empty. And Mauro Bianchi could not remember a time in his life when that had been true before.

As soon as he reached sexual maturity, he'd not been alone unless by his own choosing. As a homeless boy, he'd found quite handily that if he were to seduce a woman who did have a bed, he could get not only sex but a nice place to stay.

He had never been shy about using his body. It was one of his many tools. Something that could bring him profit and pleasure, and why not?

He behaved thus even still.

But since his encounter with Alice. Alice Steele, who he knew was not real. He had searched high and low for women bearing that name who resembled her even slightly. Women who resided in England, and then indeed anywhere, and none fit her description.

As he suspected, her name was not real.

She was like a ghost. And the only thing he had to assure himself that she had been real at all was the shoe.

The shoe that sat on his nightstand. Not the act of a man who was in his right mind. Not at all. But knowing that did not entice him to change it.

He didn't feel in the mood to be in his right mind. That was the problem.

He was in the mood for *her*. Hungry for *her*.

He'd told himself he'd never be hungry again. Never want without having.

She'd forced him into that position and it made him feel…

Powerless.

Which was a foolish thing. He was a man at the top of the world. At the top of his field. She was… She was nothing. Just a woman in a club. He was a man who'd risen from the slums of Italy in defiance of his father, a man who had been rich and titled and had wanted nothing to do with his son.

On the far wall, between the windows that overlooked a view of Rome below, news was playing on the TV. He always had news on. It was imperative that he keep up with world events, and he was well able to absorb information without giving it his full attention. His ability to multitask another part of his storied rise to success. His aptitude for numbers, and investments, and indeed for picking places that would become the hottest locations in terms of real estate and trends, had made him incredibly wealthy.

That required him to work constantly, and to pay attention to a great many details at once.

Of course, he could pay people to do much of the day-to-day things now, but still, if he didn't have a lot of input he was bored easily.

Without a female in his bed for the past three months he was growing intensely bored and incredibly bad tempered.

But no one appealed to him. None at all. None save...

Suddenly, a flash of red hair caught his attention and he gave his full focus to the TV, where a woman was sitting in a private-looking room, pale legs crossed at the ankles, hands folded in her lap. She was dressed incredibly demurely. Her red hair was pinned into an elegant bun, her butter-yellow skirt falling below her knees, her high heels sensible and sedate.

She looked so very like the woman—*his* woman—from three months ago, and yet like a different creature entirely.

She was regal in her posture, her every

movement elegant, each slight turn of her head intentional.

"Sir," Carlo said.

"Shut up," Mauro said, grabbing the remote and turning the TV up.

She was speaking, but it was in a different language, something like Norwegian, but slightly different, and he didn't speak it either way. They were not putting up subtitles on the screen, but the news commentators were going over the top in his native Italian.

"Queen Astrid von Bjornland issued a statement today to her people, that she is about to embark on an unusual path for a woman in her position. The queen is pregnant, it seems, and is determined to raise the child alone. Invoking an old rule native to the country, the queen is able to claim herself as the sole parent of the heir to the throne."

The camera panned away from the woman, shrinking the video down to a small square, where two news anchors were sitting at a desk now, a man and a woman.

"And only women can do this?" the man asked, looking somewhat incredulous.

"Yes." The female news anchor nodded gravely. "An old, protective law that ensured a queen would not be bound to one of the country's invaders, should she be forced against her will."

Against her will? She had…

That lying bitch.

She was pregnant with his child.

More than that, she was denying him his right as a father.

It took him back in an instant. To what it had been like to be a boy. Knowing his father was there in the city, an omnipresent being in his mind who had been potentially around any corner. Who had, to him, been possibly any well-dressed man walking by.

He'd known his father was a rich man. A powerful man.

A man who didn't want him.

And he had done his best to be careful—with every woman except this one—but he'd always known that with sex there was a chance birth control would fail. And he'd always known that should that ever happen he would not be like the man who'd fathered him.

He would never let a child of his wonder like that. Would never leave him abandoned, unanchored to what he was.

Would never deny him anything he had.

Yes, Astrid von Bjornland had money, had a title. But their child was more than her. That child deserved *all*, not half.

And yet there she was. Claiming his child as hers and solely hers, when both of them knew he was well involved.

He remembered the way she had looked up at him, the way she had trembled just before he'd entered her body.

"It's fine," she had whispered.

It had bloody well not been fine. He hadn't realized he'd stood up until he looked over and saw Carlo's shocked expression.

"Sir?"

"Ready my plane," Mauro said, his tone hard. "I'm leaving."

"Where are you going?"

"Bjornland. I hear it's lovely in summer, and a bit harsh in winter. However, I hear their queen is a lying snake all year round. And that is something that needs addressing."

"Mr. Bianchi…"

"Don't worry," he said. "I'm not going to make an international incident. Provided she falls in line."

CHAPTER FOUR

"WHAT THE HELL were you thinking?"

The voice boomed.

"Excellent," Latika said, her tone dripping with disdain. "His Majesty King Gunnar has arrived. Oh, wait. But he is not king, is he?"

"I still outrank *you*," Astrid's brother said, sweeping into the room, each one of his thirty-three years evident on his face thanks to years of hard living. "And lest you become confused, darling Latika, I don't covet my sister's position. In fact, I would rather die. However, I do have some opinions on how she might conduct her business."

"That's *very* fascinating," Astrid said. "Except it is not."

"Why didn't you tell me?" he asked, his tone turning fierce, and she felt momentarily bad for her anger. Momentarily.

"Because. Telling you defeats the purpose. This is no one's business but mine. And that's the entire point of it. My heir. No one else's."

"Except, there is someone, isn't there?" Gunnar asked. "I know how these things work."

"Science is a wonderful thing," Astrid said drily. "Perhaps that was the method I employed to find myself with child."

"I don't suppose you're going to tell me," Gunnar said.

"No," she responded. "But you didn't have to return to Bjornland on my account."

"I fear *very much* that I did. You have created an incident."

"You create incidents nightly, brother dear."

"I am not the heir, Astrid. And I am a man. You know that unfair as it is… It is different."

"There is no incident," Astrid insisted. "I am well within my rights to do this. I have done all of the research required to discern that."

"Father's council will oppose you. That is their function. To keep control and power, to keep traditions. To curb your power, because father believed that men were best left in charge and not women at all."

"They can try," Astrid said. "But they won't succeed. They will not, and they cannot. Don't you think, Gunnar, that I made absolutely sure I could not legally fail in this before committing?"

Gunnar shook his head. "You underestimate the power of old men who feel their traditions are being threatened."

"This is a very old law," Astrid said, looking square at her brother. They could not be more opposite in temperament. Gunnar was a risk taker. The rebel prince who spent his life skydiving out of planes, serving in the military and piloting helicopters. Who would have been perfectly at home at a club party like the one Astrid had attended only three months ago. When she had turned her world upside down, and made a choice to wrest control of her life away from the hands of those men he was talking about now.

He was like a Viking. His eyes the color of ice, his hair blond. His beard a darker gold that gave him a roguish appearance the press waxed poetic about.

The Viking Prince.

He was also her very best friend in the entire world, in spite of the fact that he was a massive pain. Latika saw him *only* as a pain, that much was clear. The feeling, it often seemed, was mutual.

"I have not underestimated anything. And I'm prepared for a fight. But there is a reason that I could let no one know before I made my announcement public. I also made sure that every media outlet was aware of the law in Bjornland. The one that protects the queen should she need to claim an heir as solely hers. Well, Latika ensured that made its way out to everyone."

"Did you?" Gunnar asked. "Just how involved with all of this were you?"

"Latika does what I ask her to," Astrid said.

Latika held up a hand and arched her dark brow. "It's all right. I don't need you to protect me from him. I have done my duty by my queen. And by this country. I may not be a citizen by birth, but I swear my allegiance, and you well know it."

"For now. Until you go back to America.

And then, all of these problems will be ours and ours alone."

"Problems that I willingly took on," she said, her tone firm. "I am a queen, I am not a child."

"Your Majesty." One of her guards rushed into the room, his expression harried. "It seems that we have an uninvited guest at the palace, and while we had thought to shoot him on sight, he is quite famous."

Astrid blinked. "I'm not sure I understand."

"A man has walked into the palace without permission," the guard clarified.

"Then why didn't you shoot him?" Gunnar asked.

"The fame," the other man said. "We would be liable to create an international incident."

"Who is it?" Astrid asked.

"Mauro Bianchi."

Astrid's stomach clenched, the blood in her veins turning to ice. There was no way. No possible way that he could know. She just didn't give him that much credit. That he would recognize her. That he would care.

"What does he want?"

"He wishes to see you."

"Now I really don't like this," Gunnar said. "Please tell me that this man was not involved in the creation of your child."

"Define *involved*," Astrid said.

"You know exactly what I mean. Don't play coy, particularly if you don't want to be treated like a child."

"The child is mine," Astrid repeated. "And mine alone."

"Please speak to him?"

"Yes," Astrid said. "I will speak to him."

"And I shall accompany you," Gunnar said.

"No," Astrid said. "I will speak to him alone."

"You're not *my* queen," Gunnar pointed out.

"I was unaware that you had become an expat of our beloved country, my dear brother."

"You are my sister," he said. "And that takes precedence over any title."

"Then as my brother I ask you to respect my wishes. The fact that men would not respect my wishes is the reason this is happening."

"I understand," he said. "I understand full well why you feel you had to do this, Astrid.

But you're not alone. You have my support, and you will have my protection."

"I don't need it," Astrid said. "I possess the power to command that he be shot on sight. Frankly, I could ask the same of you."

"Were you… Issuing an order?" her guard asked.

"Not yet." Astrid flicked a glance between her brother and Latika. "Will you please keep an eye on him?"

"I don't get paid to babysit," Latika pointed out.

"And I receive no compensation for spending time in the company of a snarling American," Gunnar bit out. "But here we are."

Astrid left, muttering about how she wouldn't have to have him shot on sight, as he and Latika were just as likely to kill each other during her absence.

She made her way out into the antechamber of the Royal Palace, her heels clicking on the marble floor. When she saw him, her stomach dropped. His impact had not been diminished by their time apart. Not in the least. In fact, if anything, her response to him was even deeper. More visceral. Possibly because she knew exactly what he could make her feel now.

"May I help you?" she asked.

He stopped and reached into his jacket, and all of the guards in the room put their hands on their weapons.

"Stand down," Astrid said. "He isn't going to shoot me."

"Not at all," he responded. Instead, when he pulled his hand out, he was holding a shoe. *Her* shoe.

"I had thought that you might possess its partner."

"I'm not sure I know what you're talking about."

"Is that so? *Alice.*"

She stiffened, straightening her shoulders. "I am Queen Astrid von Bjornland. And I do not know anyone by that name. You are mistaken, sir."

"And I am not blind. Your hair down, a bit more makeup and a bit more skin is hardly a convincing disguise, my Queen. If you wished to truly fool me you will have to try much harder than that."

Irritation crept up her spine, irritation that he was not minding what he said in front of her guards. Irritation that he was here at all.

"Leave us," she said, gesturing toward the guards.

The room cleared, every man leaving at her behest. At least she commanded authority over her own guards. There was that.

"Does every man in your life defer to you in such a manner?"

She met him full on, making her expression as imperious as possible. "Not just the men."

"I am no one's puppet," he said.

"I did not need you to be a puppet."

There was no point in lying to him. He wasn't stupid. It was entirely too clear that they had met before. And there was something... Something between them, an electricity that arced across the space. There was no pretending anymore. She simply had to find out what he wanted and provide him with that, and try to end this encounter as quickly as possible.

"I need my freedom," she said. "I am queen, and there are a great many people who don't respect my position. I did what had to be done."

"You tricked me into getting you pregnant."

"I *seduced* you. I didn't trick you. You went along with everything happily."

"You said everything was all right. You said it was fine to have sex without a condom."

"I said it was fine. And for my purposes it was. I sincerely hope that you don't treat every hookup in such a casual manner when it comes to protection."

"I don't," he said, the words gritted out through his teeth.

"Just with me, then. But still. I did not trick you. The fact that you assumed *fine* meant what you wanted it to mean and went along with it speaks to how foolish men are where sex is concerned."

As if she would have been capable of making a more rational decision in the moment.

"I want my child," he said.

"It's *my* child." Hers. Her child to love and to raise as she saw fit. To support and protect.

And give all the things her parents never had. "By law. I can declare my child fatherless, and I have done so."

"That might be a law, Queen Astrid, but it is not reality. I am the father of your child whether you speak it or not. And I am not one of your citizens."

"No. But you are in my country. Which is where my child will be born. And my child is one of my citizens."

"You underestimate me. You are so arrogant because of your position. You have no idea who you are dealing with. You feel that you face opposition? Do you truly understand what opposition is? It is not a disgruntled cough during a meeting that makes you feel as if someone might be challenging you. No. I will give you so much more than that. If you would like to learn about opposition, I will give you a study in it."

"You should know that I don't respond well to threats," she said, her tone like ice. "Indeed, I don't respond to them at all."

"You don't respond to *empty* threats. Because that is all the red-faced, posturing men that you've dealt with in the past have ever issued. But I will tell you, my Queen, my threats are never idle. They are very real. I might be a bastard of ignoble birth, but the power that I possess is very real indeed. What will the public think if I were to claim my child?"

"Why?" she asked. "It is my understanding that a man in your position will want nothing to do with the child. And that is one reason I selected you, lest you think that I meant you any harm or wanted anything from you."

"You assumed you knew what manner of man I was based on the press and what they had written about me, and that was your first mistake. Tell me, Astrid, what does the press say about you? How true is it?"

"The press has never had occasion to write about a scandal of mine. And I knew full well going into this that I was inviting that. You cannot scare me."

"You have imagined the wrong sorts of headlines, I think. I doubt what you want is a long-term custody battle looming over your head. The problem here is that you imagined me as a prop. A means to an end, but what you failed to see as you read all of those headlines, as you examine all those photos of me in the articles and imagine me touching you. Imagine me claiming that body of yours, and we both know you imagined it. That you got wet thinking of it late at night in your bed. You forgot what I am."

Astrid drew back, her heart thundering. Because he was so close to the truth, it cut her close to the heart. He wasn't wrong. She had imagined him as a chess piece. Capable of strategy, certainly, but she had also imagined that she could see ahead to every move he might make. That she understood what sort of man he was, and what he might want. But his standing here had proved already that he was not anything like she had anticipated.

She had thought of him as a barbarian, as a conqueror so many times. But in a vague, fantastical sense. In a sexual one. She had not thought in concrete terms about what it would mean to go up against this man.

Because she had not imagined he would oppose her. On that score, he was correct. She had imagined nothing like this.

She had underestimated him. And it galled her to admit it.

"What else could you want?" she said. "Anything else. I know you don't need money, and I will not insult you with such an offer. There are business opportunities to be had in Bjornland, and I am more than willing to facilitate easing the way for you. Whatever it is you want, I will give it. Only don't ask me to sacrifice this. This is what I need to claim the throne, and I will not…"

"I will not be managed. I want nothing less than what I have demanded. I want my child."

"Why?"

"Because as a boy I sat back and watched my father live in excess while my mother earned her meager pay in ways that cost. A man with money who does not care for his own is not a man at all. He is weak. Vile. The lowest form of being to ever walk the earth. If indeed you can call what he does walking. He would be better suited to crawling on his belly. I am not that man. And I will be damned if I will allow you to manipulate me. To think that I can be bought."

"What do you suggest?"

"I suggest shared custody, my Queen. But I imagine that's going to damage the optics of your little kingdom."

She blinked, not entirely certain how that would work. "There is no way that I can do that. You have to either be out of the picture entirely, the secret to the world, or you must…" Her stomach rolled. "You would have to marry me."

"Why not?" He shrugged a shoulder. "You had no intention of marrying, clearly."

"I had no intention of being maneuvered into a political marriage that wasn't of my choosing. That isn't quite the same thing."

"And yet I find in this moment the end result could likely be the same. There would be no downside to a marriage between the two of us. You can consolidate the power as you see fit, you will not be forced to marry a man chosen by this council that you're so opposed to, and I certainly have no interest in meddling in the affairs of your country."

"And you are a prime candidate for marriage?"

"Not at all. But aren't games of infidelity stock standard for royals?"

"It would require a bit more discretion than you seem capable of exhibiting."

"I can be very discreet when I choose. Tell me, my Queen. Have you seen a single headline about my sexual exploits with a virginal redhead in my private suites? No, I don't think you have. Had I wanted a headline there would have been one." He stepped forward, and tossed her shoe on the ground in front of her, the crystalline material glimmering in the light. "It seems I was able to find you without resorting to such tactics. Or trying this on any of the feet of all the eligible maidens in the country."

She thought suddenly so clearly. The queen was in check. The king had her cornered.

She could not see a way out.

"What is a queen without a king, after all?"

"According to the history of the world, more powerful."

"Not if the queen has been shamed and disgraced in the media."

Panic tightened around her throat, and as he

advanced on her, shamefully, something other than panic took hold of her. A sense of shameful, heated desire that she despised.

"I have no designs on your kingdom. What I want is to give my son or daughter validity. To ensure that they have all that is rightfully theirs. And if I benefit from having my name attached to Bjornland, and to royalty, then so be it."

"Is that what this is to you? A game?"

"That's what it was to you. The fact that you don't like the outcome of that game is not my concern. You played with me."

"Whether you think so or not, I wasn't playing with you. I was helping myself."

His expression shifted, a deadly light in those dark eyes. "Do you know what a child who was born in the gutter dreams of? What it must look like from the very top. When you are born looking up, it concerns you greatly. How it must feel to look down. I know the answer to that now. And yet, any real sense of belonging in high society escapes me. I am looked upon as a trinket often, to women who wish to slum it. A bit of rough on the side. And surely, you must know that, as you did not see me any differently. In fact, I would suggest that you thought I wasn't smart enough to find out what you had done."

He began to circle her, a wolf, a predator now, looking at her as if she was a sheep. "Did you think that somehow my impoverished, low-born eyes would not be able to recognize you when you went from common club slut to queen? What you, and all of your kind, would do well to remember is that the odds are greatly stacked against someone born in my position, and if I make it to where I am, the chances are I am much smarter than you've ever had to be. Much more determined. My patience undoubtedly greatly exceeds yours. And that means that on this score I will win. My ruthlessness exceeds yours too. Yours is all theoretical. You have no idea the things I've done to get where I am. And I don't regret a single one."

Her heart was thundering. A sick feeling invading her body. Because what could she do? He was correct. He could flay her in the media.

Expose what they had done as something seedy. Call it a one-night stand, expose the parentage of her child, and the origins of it. Or, she could take hold of it now. Say the two of them had fallen in love. Yes. A love match. She could control the narrative. She could find a way to spin it.

"You must pretend to be in love with me," she commanded.

"You've already suggested to the entire world that your child had no father. How do you profess to shift that now?"

"I will say that we had a whirlwind romance. But that I was not brave. And I was afraid that you might be rejected by the council, by my people. But in the end, you came after me, and my heart won. I will say that I trust that my people will honor what I want in my heart. We will live separate lives. We will be married only in the eyes of the law. You may conduct your affairs as you see fit as long as you do it quietly. And as long as you wait."

"Wait?"

"You will remain celibate for the first two

years of our marriage. If anyone were to get wind of the fact that you are having affairs so soon after our child was born, and so soon after I professed that the two of us had fallen in love, it would cast everything into doubt. Already having you as my husband will be an incredibly difficult thing for the nation to accept."

"More difficult than you staking your claim as an unwed mother?"

"Possibly not. But I was prepared for that fight. Because this position is one that I was born to be in. And I must fight for it daily because of my sex. And you tell me what you would have done in my situation."

"Likely exactly what you did. Though, I would have chosen someone with transparency, and paid for their silence."

She could have done that. She had thought about it. But the fact of the matter was she had seen him and become captivated. It was something that she had a difficult time admitting, because it made it clear that there was a personal element to what had occurred. That was something she didn't really wish for him to know.

That when he'd said she had thought of him at night, thought of him and become aroused, he wasn't wrong.

No. He wasn't wrong at all.

What she had done had been clouded by desire. And it was easy for her to try to pretend it had been a clinical maneuver on her part. But the inclusion of Mauro Bianchi had always been suspect. She had tried to tell herself there were many reasons apart from the fact that she wanted to touch his body. To kiss him. To have him.

Well, now she'd had him. But not in the way that she had once wished.

She was queen, and he had come into her palace. Her country. She should feel a sense of power, regardless of his threats. This was her house. Not his. And yet, all she felt was the sense that she had let a tiger inside. One that didn't care about hierarchy or blood.

One that cared only for what he might possess and how. He might exploit the weaknesses of those around him.

"You have a deal," he said. "An engagement, more accurately."

"Good," Astrid said. "That means we have a lot to do. A lot of training to prepare you for your role as consort."

"I thought you would have known by now," he said, a dangerous smile curling that wicked mouth of his. "I am not one to be trained. I am not the one who will be receiving instruction. What you will have to learn is how to be a woman who would stand at my side. A woman who would compromise her kingdom for me. At the moment, you're not believable in such a role."

She narrowed her eyes. "I don't understand the need for a farce."

"You're the one who demanded it. It isn't my fault if you didn't think about what that might mean."

He took his phone out of his pocket and pressed a number, holding it to his ear. "Carlo," he barked. "For the time being I will be relocating to Bjornland. You will have my things sent here until further notice."

Astrid bristled, trying to regain control of

the situation. "Of course you will move into the palace."

"No," he said. "I will not. When we are married, we can perhaps share the same residence for part of the year. Until then, I am more than comfortable procuring my own lodgings."

"There's no point," she said. "There's no point, everyone already knows that I'm pregnant."

"Yes, but what must be made clear, to you and everyone else, is that I am not a pet. I will have nothing to do with the day-to-day running of your country. I am not a man who needs to rent a space in a woman's bed to have a roof over his head. I am not a man you can control. You would do well to remember that."

He then turned and walked from the throne room, leaving Astrid standing there wondering how all of this had spun out of her control. It had started out as the perfect plan, and now it wasn't even her plan anymore.

Mauro Bianchi had given her many firsts.

Her first time waiting in line.

Her first time having sex.

Her first time feeling utterly and completely at the mercy of another person.

She was trapped. And she could see absolutely no way out.

CHAPTER FIVE

IT TOOK MAURO less than twenty-four hours to acquire a penthouse in the small business district of Bjornland's capital city, only three miles from the palace.

It was a simple thing to figure out a temporary work setup, where he could call in to any meeting he might be needed at over the next few weeks.

He wasn't leaving Astrid unattended. Not now. Not until everything was settled between them. Legally.

He also wasn't a dog that could be brought to heel, which was why he was refusing to move into the palace.

It took less time than that for him to acquire an engagement ring for his royal bride.

He had no doubt that she would be expecting to use a piece of jewelry belonging to the royal family, but he would not have it be so. He was not a house cat, and he would be damned if he were treated like one. That meant consolidating as much of his own power in the moment as he could. And what he had found was that there really wasn't much that couldn't be solved with money. Money was the universal way of gaining power and control. He might not have a title, and he might be theoretically beneath Astrid in this country, but he had no doubt he could buy the government of this country many times over. And he found that as long as he made it clear that was the case, people rushed to accommodate him.

He also managed to procure a reservation at what he had been assured was the queen's favorite restaurant. It was the most highly coveted in the entire country.

The next step had been ensuring that he could get the queen to the restaurant. He'd thought about kidnap, but, with as many guards as she had, it would be needlessly complicated.

He had discovered through his research that

the queen had an assistant. And he intended to use her if necessary.

He picked up the phone and waited while it rang. "Yes?"

"Is this Latika Bakshmi?"

"How did you get this number?" He could hear her lips go tight, could sense that her gaze had gone narrow and cold.

"I have connections," he said easily. "This is Mauro Bianchi. I hear that you are the minder of my new fiancée."

"She is not your fiancée. At least, not yet. As it is not printed in any papers anywhere."

"Is that the standard by which engagements are measured?"

"In this world."

"We have a verbal agreement. More than that, she is carrying my child."

"I would kill you myself to protect her," Latika said. "I hope you understand that."

He was impressed. It took real leadership to inspire that kind of loyalty. Real friendship. He had not been able to get a read on his betrothed, not in a meaningful sense, since meeting her outside of that initial encounter, when she had been pretending to be someone else entirely. She seemed frosty. Distant, and completely unlike the beautiful, witty woman he had met that night. But the fact that Latika seemed quite so dedicated to her indicated that there was something more than she had shown him. Not that it mattered either way.

None of this had anything to do with her.

Not in a personal sense. It was all about his child.

He would no sooner touch her again then he would allow a snake in his bed.

"I admire that," he said. "But I would also like to remain unmurdered. I do not want to hurt your princess. I simply want to ask her to dinner."

"You *are* hurting her," Latika said. "By pushing this marriage the way that you are."

"What do you suggest? That I allow my child to grow up without my name? Without me?"

He would not let his child grow up alone.

There was a long pause. "She didn't think you would care."

"I do," he returned. "I don't know the relationship you had with your own father, but surely you must understand that it is a loss to me to think I might not know my child."

The pause on the other end of the line was longer this time. "What exactly did you need to know?"

"I would like to take her out to dinner tonight. I was hoping you could facilitate that."

"I think that I can."

By the time Mauro pulled up to the palace that night in his newly acquired car, he had every puzzle piece in place. What he had said to her about the way that he maneuvered the press was true. If he wanted to be seen by the press, then he was. Likewise, he knew how to avoid them. He was more than happy to cultivate a certain image in the media as it suited him. And more than happy to be left alone when it suited him, as well.

Tonight he needed an audience. And he had made sure that there would be one.

The restaurant itself was built into the side of a mountain. The views it offered of the valley below, a broad swath of mist and green, made him understand why Bjornland was listed as one of the world's most pristine undiscovered gems.

Staff in the kitchen had ensured that the photographs he wished to have taken tonight would be taken. A bit of money in the right palms, and the paparazzi would be let in the back doors at the appropriate time. He was bound and determined that he would secure this union and bind Astrid to him as quickly as possible.

He did not get to where he was in life by waiting. Or by leaving anything to chance. The palace doors opened, and she appeared.

Dressed in an immaculate emerald green dress with a wide, square neck that showcased her delicious breasts. The dress skimmed her curves, falling down below her knee, hugging each line and swell of her body like a lover.

It was a shame she was so beautiful. Considering he knew exactly what she was. Even knowing, his body responded to her. That connection that he had felt from the moment he had first seen her defied any kind of logic, and it continued to do so.

A valet came to the car and opened the passenger side, and she paused before getting in.

"It is you."

"Did your faithful sidekick not tell you?"

"She did not. She was rather intentionally vague." Astrid sank down into the car with a great deal of overly dignified posture. She looked like an arched hen, stiff and tall, but visibly ruffled. "She may in fact find herself looking for a job."

"I would only hire her in my company," he said, treating her to a grin he knew was wicked. And it had the desired result. Her color mounted, her indignation increasing.

"Why would you do that?"

"She helped me. And I am loyal to those that help me. Make no mistake."

"That's interesting," she said as he put his car in Drive and roared away from the palace. "It's interesting because you have rather a reputation for treating people as if they're disposable."

"You mean women," he said, pointedly.

"Yes," she said.

"I have many women that work at my company, and they will tell you differently."

"I mean *lovers*," she clarified.

"And yet, here you are."

"That's different," she said.

"If you say so. The media makes much about my reputation, and a good portion of it is deserved. I am a man with a healthy sexual appetite, and I have never seen the point in pretending otherwise. However, I am a man from a particular background. And I learned long ago that only people with a disposable income could afford to treat others as if they were disposable. I was dependent upon the kindness of others for a great many years, and I have not forgotten it."

"But to hear the press tell it…"

"I'm ruthless," he said. "Relentless in my pursuit of the almighty dollar. And that might be true. I have thought nothing of buying property out from under the rich and titled. But I have not—and will not—send anyone to the poorhouse. I have scruples. Isn't that an inconvenient thing for you to learn?"

She said nothing.

"Does it bother you?" he pressed. "The idea that I might not be a caricature that you can easily pin down? You wanted me to be a villain, did you not? Someone that you could easily say deserved to have his child hidden from him. After all, if I am everything you seem to think, I should not have a child in my presence, should I?"

She was frozen now, that stiff posture adding to her silence.

"I am not a nice man," he continued. "On that score you are correct. I like excess. There you are correct, as well. But there are certain things that I cannot endure. That I will not abide by. I do not treat human beings like trash. Not the poor. And certainly not children. Least of all my own."

"How kind of you," she said, archly, making it clear she still found his standards of humanity beneath her.

"Do you actually want this child?" he asked as they continued up the winding mountain road that he knew would lead them to the palatial restaurant.

"Yes," she said, her tone fierce. "I want this

child very much. My life has been incredibly lonely. Filled mostly with tutors and sycophants. My brother has been my primary companion for most of that time, but he had a very different life than I did. He had a lot more freedom."

"You are the queen," he pointed out. "You have more power than he does."

"More power in this case is not more freedom. I'm five minutes older than my brother," she said. *"Five minutes.* My brother is everything the old men of my father's council could possibly want in a leader. A tall, strapping man. An alpha male with the kind of immediate presence that gives a sense of confidence and intimidation. And me?" She shrugged. "I'm a woman. But, if not for a little bit of acrobatics in the womb, they would have the leader they wanted, and not the one they're stuck with. Do you have any idea how much that galls them? How much they resent it? I can feel it every time I'm in their presence. And make no mistake, a great many citizens of this country feel the same way. When my father passed away, I think they all hoped that there would be some secret switch. That I would abdicate. That I would do the right thing. That is what some people think. That it would be right for me to abdicate because of my gender. I have been above reproach all this time. And I have been opposed every step of the way for no other reason than that I was born a woman. It was my mother's deepest wish that I would not allow them to take what was rightfully mine. And I have not. I will not."

"And the child… The child helps you accomplish this."

"The issue of me needing a husband was being pushed. And there was a possibility that they would have the right to select a husband for me. There is also a great deal of responsibility placed on the production of an heir. Once I have produced one, some of the council's oversight is removed. This is a protective method that has been in place in the country for generations. To ensure that a royal is doing their duty by the country, and if not, then decisions may have to be made."

"And there is some arcane law that says the

queen can be considered solely responsible for her own issue."

"Yes." She sighed heavily. "It seemed the smartest thing to do."

"It might've been," he said. "Had you chosen any other man."

"Do you know what I liked about you?" she asked. He heard a slight smile in her voice.

"No," he returned. It was true, he didn't. Based on his interactions with her he would have assumed she liked nothing about him at all.

"You reminded me of a warrior. I liked that about you. I thought… That is the kind of genetic material I need for my child. And you might judge that, I understand. But it made sense to me at the time. I was feeling a bit desperate."

He let silence lapse around them for a moment. The only sound that of the tires on the road, the engine a low hum running beneath. "The problem with warriors," he said finally, "is that you cannot control all that they might do."

She laughed. A small, humorless sound.

"Understood. Understood all too well at this point."

It was then that they reached the summit of the mountain, the restaurant glittering against the stone.

"Oh," she breathed. "This is my favorite."

"Good," he said, and he fought against the strange curl of pleasure in his stomach that he had pleased her in some way.

There were glittering Christmas lights around the perimeter of the restaurant, green boughs hanging heavily over the doors and windows.

"It's a bit early for all of this," he commented.

"Perhaps," she agreed. "But it's nice all the same."

She softened a bit, talking about Christmas. It confounded him. He didn't much understand the joy of Christmas.

He'd never had a Christmas, not really.

They left the car with the valet, and he looped his arm through hers as he led her into the restaurant. She was like ice beside him, but he didn't pay attention to that. Instead, he leaned in, his lips brushing against her ear.

"You will have to look as if you enjoy touching me."

"I didn't realize this was an exhibition."

"You are Queen Astrid von Bjornland, and I am Mauro Bianchi, the most famous self-made billionaire in all the world. Everything we do is an exhibition."

"Most famous?" she asked drily. "You think very highly of yourself."

"I didn't realize that ego and honesty were considered the same thing in your world."

"I consider ego very important. Never think that I'm insulting you for pointing out that you have a healthy one. After all, I'm the queen that millions think should not have a crown. How do you think I walk with my head held so high?"

"Well, now," he said. "That I can respect."

"Whatever you think about me," she continued. "I guarantee that you don't have the first idea of what it means to operate in my world. You might be rich. But you don't understand the expectations that have been placed on me. No one does. My brother… He tries. It cannot be said he doesn't. He is my twin, and the closest person to me in the entire world. But he can't fully understand. I don't know that a man ever could."

"Is that so?"

"Yes. Now, I imagine that being of low birth, as you are—"

"Low birth," he said. "What a delicate way to phrase it."

She shrugged. "I wasn't trying to be delicate in particular. But being from the kind of station you are, I imagine that you reached some opposition when you were trying to ascend. I also imagine that once you proved yourself capable, then it was assumed you were capable."

"I confess, my prowess has never been called into question. In any arena."

"I was born to this," she said. "My blood runs blue. My education, my upbringing… It was all geared toward me finding success in this career that I was born for. And yet whether or not I am capable of handling it… My marital status, whether or not I'm carrying an heir, all of those things, seem to matter more. I am a pass-through ruler. And believe me when I tell you they will all pray this child is a boy."

"England seems to have done all right for itself," he pointed out.

"It isn't the same. Our country is smaller, the government is run differently. We don't have parliament."

"Let us go inside," he said.

They were standing out in the chilly air, Astrid looking up at him, and he had a feeling that she was putting off the moment that they would have to go in and face the public. But then, she had no idea the level of public that would be in attendance.

"All right," she said slowly.

She allowed him to lead her into the restaurant, and he knew that he was being allowed. After all, this woman did not seem to cow under any threat or circumstance. Whether or not the council respected all that she was, he did. He could see what she was. It oozed from her every pore. From the very way in which she carried herself.

He moved his hand to her lower back as they walked into the warm restaurant. It was very Scandinavian, with a sparse design aesthetic, the windows looking out over the impressive mountain view, the trees inky and black against the backdrop of the rich velvet sky, the stars glittering like diamonds.

"This is a beautiful place," he commented, keenly aware of the fact that all of the eyes in the room had turned to them.

"Yes," she said, somewhat absently. "It truly is."

He leaned in, conscious of the fact that they would be being photographed now. "And what is your favorite thing on the menu?"

"I always get the special," she said. "Whatever is seasonal. Oh, and if there's an appetizer with one of the Bjornish aged cheddars, I always get that."

"You have a fondness for cheese?"

"I would distrust anyone who doesn't."

"I see. So that is how you arrive at conclusions regarding who you can trust and who you can't? Which foods they have an affinity for?"

"I've yet to surmise a more adequate way of parsing a person's character.

"Well," he said, "I like cheese. What does that say about your metric?"

She looked at him, those lovely, green eyes appraising. "I chose you, didn't I?"

The words were cool and unsettling. They made him feel much more like she might be in the driver's seat than he was comfortable with.

The maître d' appeared and quickly ushered them to a semiprivate table, which Mauro liked because it gave the appearance that they were attempting to stay out of the way, while still allowing for the paparazzi to be able to get discreet photos.

In his experience, the quality of the publicity was all in how you courted it. Or how you appeared not to.

And just like that, he was reminded of who was in control.

At least tonight.

She was a fascinating woman in some ways. He was not accustomed to dealing with women—with anyone—who had even a comparable amount of power to his own. Astrid was a queen, and the idea that she could snap her fingers and have him executed infused him with a particular kind of fascination he had not dealt with before.

He hadn't anticipated a powerful woman being quite such an aphrodisiac, and yet it made sense. What good was strength and power if it went untested? What good was strength and power when pitted against someone weaker?

Far more interesting to spar with an equal.

When a waiter appeared, Mauro spoke quickly to him, procuring the specials, and requesting a special appetizer with local cheese for the queen.

"You did not have to order for me," she said.

"Perhaps not," he said. "But I thought it might make an interesting challenge." He looked at her. "You did not have to let me order for you. I imagine you could have stopped me at any point."

"It's true," she bit out.

"I imagine that you could call the waiter back now and reverse my order if you find it unsatisfactory."

She sniffed. "Well, you got what I would have ordered anyway."

He smiled. "That isn't true."

"Oh, yes?"

"Yes. It isn't true because you would never have asked for a special entrée to be made for you."

She sniffed again. "I told you, I was raised to be a queen. Why do you think that is beyond my scope?"

"Because you were raised to be very careful. That is something else I know."

"It's true. My mother always stressed that I would be scrutinized much more closely than a potential king would be. It's impossible for me to know if it would have been different for Gunnar if he were the heir. But he gets much more leeway in the press, and his behavior is considered something of a national pastime. Of course, he is not in immediate line to the throne. So perhaps that's the reason why. But it really is impossible to know."

"I imagine you could never risk looking overly commanding."

"No," she said. "Neither could I... Neither could I ever risk dancing too close to a man."

"And so you disguised yourself in something unsuitable and went to my club?"

"The truly amazing thing," she said, "is that

people don't look closely at other people. We never search for the unexpected. I've never put a foot out of line, and so no one would ever think that they might spot me at your club. Least of all wearing the dress I had chosen. It was the perfect moment to engage in a small rebellion."

"It was coup in many ways, it could be argued."

"I suppose. To claim the power that should've been mine all along."

The two of them began to eat in silence and Mauro became aware of the sound of a camera. It was subtle, but it was evident, and he made sure to reach out and brush his fingertips across Astrid's knuckles. She startled, drawing her hand back.

"Your Majesty," he said. "Never make the mistake of thinking that we might not be in the presence of an audience."

"An audience?"

"I made sure the press knew that we were here."

She went still, as if she'd transformed into a pillar of salt, the stony expression on her face one of biblical proportions. "What are you up to?"

"Did you honestly think that I called you here without a plan?"

"I suspected that we would discuss these things together." She said the words through tight lips, her expression serene, even as the waves emanating from her were not.

"Smile," he said.

As if on cue, she did so, and to anyone observing them it would seem that they were having a friendly exchange.

"This is not your show," he continued. "That is one thing you need to learn about me. I am subject to no one and nothing. Least of all you. You made a choice. You stepped into my world. And now, you have ensured that you'll never fully be free of me. This was your decision, not mine. And now, here I am. I am the thing you must contend with. You assume that your consequence would be carrying my child. No, my Queen. *I* am your consequence."

"Damn," she said, keeping that smile stretched wide. "A consequence I had not foreseen. How unusual."

"Indeed."

And he knew that his next move was one she had not seen coming either. It would be cliché to wait for dessert. The move of a man who was calculating the entire event. But he was determined to make it look as if theirs was a spontaneous proposal. If this was what she wanted, the look of love, the look of a real couple, then he would give it to her. But he would give it to her on his terms. If she thought that she could be in charge of creating their narrative, she was about to be sadly disappointed.

He reached into his jacket pocket, and he produced a small ring box.

The shock on her face was not manufactured. Not in the least. It was clear to him that she had not been expecting this. Not at all. And it gave him an illicit rush, a thrill, to have her at his mercy. Because that night when he had first met her, he had felt a connection between the two of them that he had never felt with another woman before. And she had been using him.

That that bothered him at all was laughable. It shouldn't. And yet, it did. His every emotion tangled up in this thing that he had neither anticipated, nor ever thought to protect himself from.

And then it had turned out the connection was a creation. All a part of a tactical war she was waging, unbeknownst to him. He did not handle such things well.

And now, it was her turn. Her turn to be caught off guard.

He dropped to one knee in front of her, a position that she probably saw men in often, but this was not a pose of submission. Not a gesture of deference on his part.

He opened up the ring box, the piece that he was presenting her a true marvel of design. Clean and simple, like this restaurant that she favored so much. Something that reminded him of what she had worn the night they had met. A creation designed to complement who she was, rather than adding unnecessary adornment.

A large, square cut diamond, clear and bright, in a platinum setting.

Something that worked with the lines of her elegant hand, rather than overwhelming them.

"Queen Astrid," he said. "Would you do me the honor of becoming my wife."

It was not a question. And she seemed to know it.

He could sense the electricity around them, the entire restaurant now rapt at the scene in front of them. Shutters were going off, cameras raised, while people snapped completely obvious cell phone photographs of the moment. And now he had her. Now he truly had her.

"Yes," she said, her answer wooden, stiff. "Of course I'll marry you."

Her smile was effortless, the result of years of practice and breeding, he could only assume. And to anyone else she would look positively joyful.

But he could feel her rage.

Her desire to make him pay.

And it only fueled that damnable fire in his veins.

"You've made me the happiest man in the world," he said.

Then he grabbed her hand and tugged them both to their feet, drawing her up against his chest and gripping her chin between his thumb and forefinger.

The look in her eyes, that glinted there, threatened to cut him. But her actions remained agreeable.

For a woman for whom reputation was everything, this was a hostage situation. And as a man who didn't care at all what anyone thought, it was a victory.

Then, he lowered his head, and claimed her mouth with his own.

And that was the moment he had not planned for.

He hated this woman. Despised the way that she had deceived him, used him. The way that she had been intent upon hiding his child from him.

But this remained. This spark.

The electricity of the room wasn't simply coming from the excitement of the spectators around them. No. The electricity was in them. Arcing between them with uncontrollable sparks.

He wanted to devour her. Part her lips and

slide his tongue against hers. Luxuriate in this until it consumed them both.

And it was that feeling. The sense of being out of control. Of wanting…

That was what pulled him back. Because he would be damned if he would crave a thing that was out of his reach ever again.

He pulled himself away from her, staring down in triumph at her swollen mouth, her stunned expression.

"I believe this makes you my fiancée."

And just like that, he had the queen in check.

CHAPTER SIX

"How dare you make a move like this without consulting the council."

"Which move?" Astrid asked as she faced down the long board table of very angry men. Men her father had appointed to their positions over the course of his rule. It was traditional for the monarch of Bjornland to have consult of a council. With more freedom being handed over to the ruler after marriage, or after an heir was produced.

But the way this particular council had been established, without her approval, even as her reign was approaching, and with life terms given to those who sat in their positions, was unheard of. And allowed only, she imagined, because she was a woman.

Her father had installed babysitters for her.

He'd never cared that she'd done nothing but

demonstrate her ability. He couldn't see past what he considered her fundamental flaw. She was female, and would therefore be a weaker ruler. Inclined to lead with her emotions. To be swayed by her hormones in a way a man was never led about by the member of his body.

The very idea sent Astrid into a small internal rage.

Men were always so concerned with what women might do during a certain time of the month, and yet they were slaves to the whims of the lower halves of their bodies at all times of every month.

That her father had considered her weak and fallible because of her sex was, in her mind, a sign of the weakness in him.

But with her upcoming marriage, and the baby coming, they were on the way to becoming less powerful, and they were certainly sitting there looking as though they knew it.

"The one where I decided that I would be taking control of the child that I carry, or the one where I got engaged?"

"Either," Lars, the lead councilman, replied.

"Both are done," she said causally. "There's nothing to discuss."

She had whiled away her time letting these men occupy their seats. Not making waves. So that when she had the moment to consolidate her power they would be blindsided. And that was clearly what had occurred.

She would remain calm even now. Better to have them unable to anticipate her next moves.

To the outside world it might appear as if she was taking orders. As if she was allowing herself to be walked on.

But she had the trump card. And she refused to waste energy flailing when she was in the process of succeeding in a tactical strike.

The ring on her left hand felt heavy. And her lips still felt tingly from the kiss she had shared with Mauro at the restaurant. Perhaps *share* was too strong of a word. That kiss had been a conquering. Truly, the barbarian had reached the gates, and no amount of planning on her part had been sufficient to keep it from being so.

She had handed him the keys to her kingdom. She might as well tilt her head back and let him slit her throat.

And if it were ancient times, perhaps that's what would have been done. At least, after she had produced his issue.

But he claimed that he wanted nothing to do with the kingdom specifically, and right now, looking at all of the faces staring back at her, feeling the rage emanating from them, she could only take comfort in the fact that the only people more upset about this development than she, were them.

As much as she could feel her plan spinning out of control, she imagined that they could feel their control on the kingdom slipping out of their grasp.

And as long as that was the case, she would be happy enough.

"He is the father of your child?" Lars pressed.

"That is the question on the lips of everyone in the world at the moment, it seems," she said, keeping her expression serene and her shoulders straight.

"You claimed there was no father," another of the men said from the other end of the table.

"Well, I think we all know that's a lie. Even men such as yourselves don't spring from holes in the ground. They are made the typical way." She received raised eyebrows in return for that statement. "Do not all of you go looking so shocked that I am a woman. After all, if I were not, you would not be here, with the layers of additional power my father bestowed upon you. To protect myself I was willing to invoke that particular law written in our books. But it turns out, I didn't have to. The issues that Mauro and I were having—personal issues—have been resolved. And now we will be able to present a united front for the kingdom. I fail to see how this is not a winning proposition for the entire nation."

"A playboy," a dissenting voice said. "And one from the gutter at that. He is well beneath you, and beneath this kingdom."

"Is he?" she asked, with no small amount of ice in her voice. "Have I not lowered the kingdom sufficiently to reach his level? I should think that by mere virtue of the fact that I am a woman, I would have slipped us down several ranks in your estimation. Not to mention my very nonsecretive pregnancy, which the whole world knows occurred out of wedlock."

"My Queen," Lars said. "You know that you have nothing but support from the council. That is why your father solidified our position before his death. To make sure that we could support you."

"Support. Undermine. In the grand scheme of things is there any difference? I knew that in order to claim my independence I had to either marry or produce an heir. Handily, I will be able to do both very soon."

"How soon shall the marriage take place?"

"Two weeks," she said, the words, the commitment, sending a stab of terror through her body. She had not discussed this with Mauro. But she imagined that the sooner the better as far as he was concerned. After all, he had taken control of the timeline by making their engagement so visible, and thrusting it upon her without giving her any time to be coordinated. He could hardly get angry at her for keeping up with that push forward.

Well, maybe he could. But maybe it would do him some good to be angry.

She had the terrible feeling that she was going from one battle of wills straight into another. She also had the terrible feeling that the council wasn't going to go quietly.

She suddenly had the distinct vision of being pulled between Mauro and the table full of councilmen.

She also had the clear vision of Mauro being able to pull her away from all of them.

She disliked that.

She had intended to rescue herself. The idea of needing his help was galling indeed.

"That is impossible," her largest dissenter said, rubbing his hand over his face. "You know we cannot coordinate a wedding in that time."

"Then don't coordinate it. I assume you don't want a heavily pregnant queen wandering down the aisle, which means expedience should be welcome. And if that's too difficult for you, I will arrange it myself. It will coincide with the tree lighting, and other Christmas festivities Bjornland will be celebrating, and I can think of nothing better."

"You will add unnecessary duties to the staff at this time of year?" Lars sneered.

"Not at all. I will boost the economy and provide with it extra money for the season. And I am well able to ensure it all goes to plan without involvement of anyone in this room."

"How?"

"I have an assistant for a reason. And believe me, she is more efficient than this group of people all on her own. If the idea of helping to coordinate this wedding intimidates you, then I'm certain that Latika will happily take up the banner."

"This is *unprecedented*."

"That's fine. I don't mind being unprecedented in this manner, as I am unprecedented in every other way. You were the only ones that seem to have an issue with that. You are beginning to drag down the entire country."

"Mark my words," one of the men in the back said. "If the country is to fall, it will be on your head."

She firmed her jaw, calling on all the strength

she'd spent her life culminating. "Then so be it. But it will not be my head alone, but my new husband's, as well. You will find he is nothing but a staunch supporter of me. You might be able to oppose me, but when I am joined with him I will only be stronger. Two are better than one. And the two of us will be vastly better than twelve," she said, looking at them all meaningfully. "I will send you an invitation to the wedding if you wish. Otherwise, you may take a backseat. You will have to get used to that."

On that she turned on her heel and walked out of the room, listening with satisfaction as each step echoed loudly around her.

She had been angry at Mauro last night about what he had done. She had been uncertain with how to proceed. But she knew now. Everything had a purpose now.

Suddenly, this marriage actually seemed like the best idea.

It might never be a real marriage. She didn't need it to be a real marriage.

He would be a figurehead, and she... She

would finally be able to be the queen that she was always meant to be.

Dinner that night was at the palace, and it was filled with pronouncements. Mostly made *at* him. Mauro wasn't used to such things, and he found he had limited patience for it.

Though there was something exceptionally alluring about Astrid, even when she was being a pain in his ass.

Sometimes, especially when she was being a pain in his ass, and he didn't fully understand that.

"We are to be married in time for the tree lighting in the palace. It will be integrated into the ceremony in point of fact."

"Is that so?"

"How pregnant did you expect I should look on the day of our wedding, for all the papers to see?"

For some strange, inexplicable reason the idea of her looking pregnant—her stomach round with his child—did something to him that he could not explain. Something he didn't want to explain, even to himself.

"How pregnant you are or aren't when you walk down the aisle doesn't matter to me," he said. "The only reputation I have to maintain is one of total debauchery and general disdain for social niceties. For me, this is on brand."

"How nice for you," she said, drily. "We will marry in a month."

"When do you suppose you will learn I don't respond well to commands?"

"I don't know. I suspect we have a lifetime to discover that."

"Surely not a whole lifetime," he said. "Only while the child is…a child, I'd assume. Do we really need to be so pedantic that we stay together for eighteen years?"

"I hadn't considered it," she said, her expression bland. "Marriage, to me, is forever, but it certainly doesn't have to mean together."

"Elaborate," he said. "I am not from a household that contained a marriage. My view of it is limited to sitcoms and crime dramas. Both give a very different idea of what it means to be married. I imagine the truth lies somewhere between happy hijinks and murder."

Astrid chuckled softly, pushing food around

on her plate. "Yes, something like that. I think that middle ground is called 'quiet disdain.'"

"Speaking of your parents' marriage?" he asked.

"Yes. You know, my father never wanted me to be queen. My mother was stubborn about it from the beginning. From making sure the announcement that the press received was unambiguous about which child was born first."

"But he was the king. Couldn't he override her decision?"

"Yes," she said. "He could have. There were many reasons he didn't. That he would suffer in the eyes of his people, and the world, being a large part of that. Also... He knew I wasn't incompetent. If I had been I think he wouldn't have hesitated to have Gunnar named the official successor to the throne. My father wasn't an easy man, but he had a strong sense of duty. I don't know that he... I don't know that he loved anyone. But he loved the country. As for my mother..."

"Did she love him?"

"I don't think she did. Mostly they spent their marriage sleeping with other people, once Gunnar and I were born. Heir and spare in one go. Exceedingly handy."

"Before your idea to circumvent the council, what was your thought on who you might marry?" He didn't know why he was curious. He shouldn't be. Not about this minx who had upended his whole life, forcing him into a situation he didn't want to be in.

No, he didn't want to want this child. But he did.

His mother was dead now, gone. Years of hard living having taken their toll on her. Installing her in a luxury penthouse for the last six months of her life had probably extended her time on earth, but not by as much as he'd hoped.

His father still lived, but he'd vowed he'd never speak to the man again.

The child, his child, would be a real flesh-and-blood connection he could have here on this earth. This child was something real to care about. To want to care for.

He didn't…want to need those things, and yet he found he did. It was more than just a feeling of responsibility. It was something that called to a deeper place inside him.

One he'd done a great job pretending wasn't there for the past thirty-five years of his life.

Just another reason to find Astrid enraging.

But he found he was still curious.

"I didn't think about it," she said. "I imagined my parents would be involved in helping curate a selection of acceptable suitors. But they never did. My father died when I was twenty-nine. I still don't know why he didn't try to marry me off before then. A year ago, I thought of this plan. Oh, I hadn't chosen you specifically but I had decided I would have a baby alone."

"You never wanted love?"

She lowered her head, shaking it slightly. Then she laughed. "All I ever wanted was for the people around me to see that I was competent. Not in spite of being a woman. Not barely acceptable when they could have had a man. But qualified. A passionate leader, a good leader. One who loves her country and all of its people. Fantasies of romantic love have never factored into my life. I can't even get respect, why would I hinge any great thing on love?"

He could relate to that feeling, though his was not a sense he did not deserve love, but the deep, abiding belief it did not truly exist.

Love, in his mind, was an illusion. When life became bleak, love was always the first thing to crumble. In the end, people would always choose themselves. They would not choose another person. Not really.

It didn't make him sad anymore to know that. As a boy, it had. He'd been convinced if only his father could love his mother, they would be a family and be happy. He'd been convinced that if only his father would meet him, he would love him and he would want to give him and his mother the money they needed to live.

But his father loved himself. He loved the life he had in the palazzo on the hill with his wife and their real children. The children he'd made intentionally, with the aristocrat woman he'd chosen. Not the gutter trash he'd knocked up during a dalliance.

His mother had made it very clear where

she'd stood in his father's eyes. Never to make him feel sorry for her. Never to cry about injustice.

Only to make it known why any reconciliation was impossible.

Still, he'd always thought it could be so as a boy.

He'd found out as a young man he'd been wrong.

"What about you?" she asked. "Am I interrupting any marital plans?"

"No," he said. "I intended to whore my way around the world. I intend to continue doing so when our need for total discretion is resolved."

"Excellent," she said, though her tone sounded quite crisp.

"Does it bother you?"

She shook her head. "Not at all. You recall I intended to walk away from you and never see you again. I hardly intended to own your sexuality for the rest of your life. I intended to forget your name."

He smiled. "And now, here we are."

"What *the hell* is happening?"

He turned to look, at the same time Astrid

nearly gave herself whiplash twisting around when a large man, who had slightly different coloring, with blond hair and a beard, but was identical to her in the stubborn set of his jaw, came striding into the formal dining room.

"It's five in the evening, Gunnar," Astrid said, as she recovered herself. "I hope you didn't get out of bed so long before your typical wake-up time just to question my life decisions."

"I'm questioning *his*," Gunnar said, the anger in his expression making abundant sense now that he knew for sure this was Astrid's brother.

"Your sister is having my baby," Mauro said. "What precisely should I have done to treat her in a more respectful manner? I have proposed marriage to her."

"And you'll get your hands on the kingdom?" Astrid's brother was like a very large, angry Viking barreling down on him, and if he weren't an accomplished street fighter, he might have been concerned for his safety.

"Whatever your plan is… It is not going to succeed," the other man continued. "Astrid is much stronger than that."

"I'm aware of that. It's one reason I'm so fond of her."

"Your stories are conflicting," Gunnar said. "My sister made it very clear there was no father of her child. Then suddenly, you appeared."

"We had a disagreement. That disagreement has been resolved."

"It's a political marriage," Astrid said, sounding tired. "There's no point lying to him. Neither of us can get away with lying to each other ever. It's one of the worst things about having a twin."

"You don't have to do this," Gunnar said.

"I do," she insisted. "I overplayed my hand and I lost. But now we have a scenario that helps me in the end."

"In what sense?" Gunnar asked.

"The council is madder at me than you are," she said, her mouth lifting up into a small smirk.

"That is something," Mauro said.

"I assume," Gunnar said, turning his focus to Mauro, "there are official documents that can be drawn up and kept secreted away in your personal vaults well away from Bjorn-land?"

"Of course," Mauro said. "Discretion is key in my line of work."

"I didn't know *discretion* was part of your vocabulary," Gunnar said.

"Because you've never gotten wind of a single thing that I appeared to be obscuring. I find hiding in plain sight is often the best plan."

Astrid's brother regarded him with what appeared to be grudging respect.

"Now that you're through treating me like a child…" Astrid said.

"Yes, I'm sure that if I appeared with a random fiancée you'd take it in your stride."

"Of course not," Astrid said. "I'd renounce her as a gold digger."

"Then don't expect me to sit back and allow you to make choices I find…deeply suspicious."

Mauro leaned back in his chair. "You should find it deeply suspicious. Though, as I said, I have no designs on your country."

"What do you have designs on?"

Mauro leveled a gaze at the other man. "Is it so difficult to believe it's your sister?"

Gunnar shook his head once. "Not at all. But there are easier women in the world to be with. My sister has an obligation first to her country. My sister will never be able to take her husband's name, or be his housewife."

"What a happy thing, then, that my name means less than nothing to me. I am a bastard son of a whore. My name is dirt in civilized circles. But I do have money. And money allows me to go where I like, to get what I like. Better still, I have no house. A series of penthouses, yes. Private apartments nestled in exclusive clubs. But nowhere one would expect a wife to put on a twinset and pearls and… bake. My lodgings are reserved for more exotic uses."

"You may have to childproof them soon enough."

Astrid's response to that was to treat her brother to an evil glare. But she said nothing. She was a strong woman and certainly more than capable of speaking up in a situation like this and yet now she chose to remain silent.

He could only assume there was a reason. One that had nothing to do with being intimidated.

"My clubs are no place for children. But then, that is another issue. I want my child. Is that so hard to believe?"

"Most men of your sort do not."

"Then they are not men," he said. Simple. Hard.

And that seemed to earn him the most respect of all.

Eyes that were like chips of ice appraised with a coldness that would have sent a lesser man running from the room. Then finally, Gunnar turned his focus back to his sister. "Proceed with planning your wedding, Astrid, by all means. I won't stop you."

"You *couldn't*," Astrid pointed out. "I command an army."

The corner of her brother's mouth tipped up in defiance, and at that moment he could truly see that they were twins. "I said I *won't* stop you. Not that I can't. My choice of words was no accident."

"Then we're all on the same page," Mauro

said. "Including those of us who had no choice in the matter."

After that Mauro had the feeling that whatever other obstacles might rise up in the future, his brother-in-law wouldn't be one of them.

"It's actually a good thing you're getting married so quickly," Latika said, staring appraisingly at Astrid in her close-fitting lace gown.

"And why is that?" Astrid asked.

"Because this dress would no longer fit you if you waited even another week. It's getting snug as it is."

"I'm pregnant," Astrid sniffed.

The word sent a sudden jolt through her.

Words like *heir* made it all detached. But the fact remained she was going to be a mother and no matter how much she wanted to be, the reality of it felt weighty, and infused with the weight of the unknown.

But then, everything in her world felt inverted right now and there was no finding normal. Mauro was… He was a presence even when he wasn't in the palace. He had committed to working mostly in Bjornland until the wedding, leaving only a couple of times, and even then never staying overnight. He had a residence in town but she swore she could feel him.

And the feeling was...

It was electric and it was unsettling.

She wanted him. And there was no room in this situation for want. Especially when he was a brick wall she couldn't read.

He didn't seem to want her at all.

The night of the engagement he'd kissed her, and then he'd pulled away like nothing had happened while her entire body had continued to burn like a wildfire had been set off in her belly, spreading out over everything.

They could talk, and it felt cordial, but even that seemed...calculated.

She'd come closest to knowing the man the night she'd met him in his club, of that she was certain.

With no names, and no truth, she'd seen pieces of the real Mauro somehow.

He wasn't giving her any of that now.

He asked her questions. He shared his own

information with an easy defiance. As if he enjoyed his disreputable history, and lived to shock people with it.

But none of it was real.

None of it was what existed on the other side of a wall she shouldn't even want to scale.

He had been a means to an end. He continued to be.

The world was agog over their union, but they'd quickly recovered from her declaration that her child had no father becoming a shock engagement. Mostly because, more than anything, the world wanted a love story.

Even if it was improbable and unbelievable.

Maybe most especially then.

"I wasn't insulting you," Latika said.

Astrid looked at the wall, refusing to look at her assistant. "It sounded like it."

"Well, I wasn't." She tilted her head to the side, her glossy black hair sliding over her shoulder. "You truly will make a magnificent bride."

"I don't care about that. I want to be a magnificent *queen*."

Latika sighed. "You're already that. You

don't need a husband to make it true. Even if you need one to help insulate you."

"Somehow this is starting to feel a little bit like the forced marriage I was avoiding."

"Except…" Latika trailed off, as if she thought better of what she'd been about to say.

"What?"

"You've already slept with him," she pointed out. "You *are* attracted to him."

"It isn't a factor now," Astrid said, her cheeks getting warm.

"Isn't it?"

"No," she scoffed. "He's no longer interested in me anyway."

"Why do you think that?"

"He's… Well, he's completely cold toward me, and anyway…" She sighed. "I don't know. I don't know what I want from this. What I want to do. What would you do?"

Latika blinked. "Do you mean in this exact situation? Because I don't think I can answer that."

"Okay," Astrid said slowly. "I grant you that my current situation is a little bit unorthodox."

Latika snorted. "A little bit?"

Astrid turned around, facing her assistant instead of the mirror. "What do you do with men? I don't have any experience with them. Except for that one night. And I hardly think that counts."

Latika sighed heavily. "I can't say as I have any brilliant suggestions on how to handle a man like Mauro."

"But surely you must have some idea how to handle men?"

Astrid could see Latika decide to dodge the question. While she valued that skill in Latika when it came to her acting as a shield between Astrid and the rest of the world, it was deeply annoying at the moment.

"Latika, we don't speak overly much of your past because I can see that it hurts you, but if you could offer me some insight…"

"I can't. I always knew I would be married off to a man I didn't love, and I was sheltered from men to…preserve me. When the man my father chose turned out to be an ancient European with a reputation for treating women ill… Well, now I am here. I know how to plan and organize any event, how to make casual conversation with people from all walks of life. I might have been roped off from having my own social life, but I was forced to participate in the social lives of my parents. I've planned your wedding, but I can't help you here, I'm afraid."

"If nothing else, it's very helpful to have you. To have a friend."

Latika treated her to a small smile. "What is it you want from him? Because it seems to me that while you might have failed in the first iteration of your plan, this one is going to work just fine."

"That's the problem," Astrid said. "I'm really not sure what I want. I should want to keep things compartmentalized. We have a good agreement. We really do."

"But..."

"There's no *but*," she said quickly. "Not really."

Latika sighed. "You have a crush on him. You have ever since you saw his picture in that magazine."

Astrid sputtered. "One cannot have something so...benign as a crush on a man like

Mauro Bianchi. Anyway. I'm a queen. Queens don't have crushes."

"You're human. A human woman. You would have to be blind not to notice his appeal."

"So you've noticed it, then."

Latika laughed. "International playboys aren't really my thing."

"No. If they were you might not want to pinch my brother's head off every time you were in the same room with him."

Latika shifted. "Maybe."

"I need to stay strong with him," Astrid said. "I need to make sure that I don't blur lines between us."

"If you think so," Latika returned.

"You think I should do differently?"

"I wouldn't dare question you. But mostly… I had a high-handed…unorthodox upbringing, you could say. I was very cloistered, and protected. Something I know you understand. Even now sometimes I feel like I'm hiding. If I had the ability to claim freedom the way that you did, I would take it. And I know that I was a little bit disapproving of your entire plan, but it was only because I worried for you."

"So you think that I should continue on with a physical relationship with him?"

Latika shrugged. "If not him then with someone. But it seems to me that you have feelings for him. Also, you're pregnant with his baby and marrying him, so it seems that he's the most convenient target around."

"He hates me," she said. She was suddenly very aware of exactly what that strange emotion she could feel vibrating beneath the surface of the man was. "He really does. And he wants the child, and I don't understand why. I mean, he says it's because it's a man's responsibility to be a father…"

"And you don't believe him?"

"I just think there's more." She shook her head. "It's the strangest thing. It isn't that I think he's lying. Just that I can sense there's something else. And he's never going to tell me."

"Have you asked him?"

"Why would I ask him? I just said I'm fairly certain he hates me."

"You should ask him about that too. About whether or not he actually hates you. It seems to me that he could have taken a much more extreme tactic with you than he has."

"Oh, than forcing me into marriage?"

"You have to admit, as things go... His version of forcing you into marriage is fairly kind."

"*Kind* is not the word I would use for it."

"Okay. Maybe that was an overstatement. But he isn't after your country. He isn't after any of your power. And you have to admit that when compared to basically every other man in your life—except for Gunnar—that's fairly significant."

"That might be the first nice thing I've ever heard you say about my brother."

Latika rolled her eyes. "Well, it's not going to happen again. Don't get used to it."

"I'm getting married." A sick feeling settled in the pit of her stomach. She couldn't even blame morning sickness. "I wonder what my mother would think of all this."

"She would be proud of you," Latika said. "I didn't know her, but from everything you've told me I think she would approve greatly. Think of all she did, the way she put her marriage in jeopardy to ensure your position on the throne. She would understand why you were doing all of this."

Astrid had nothing else to anchor her. Nothing that made her feel particularly assured, or like she even knew which way was up. But if she could just imagine her mother being proud. It was the one thing she'd worked for all these years, really. And even if she'd never get the words of approval she'd always longed for, she knew that she was doing what her mother had always wanted her to do.

That she was becoming what her mother had wanted her to be.

For now, that would be enough.

And the mystery of Mauro, and the problem of what she was going to do about him, would have to wait to be solved.

However, the countdown to the wedding night was ticking down... And she imagined she would have to make a decision before then.

CHAPTER SEVEN

MAURO HAD NEVER given much thought to the Christmas season. As a child it had meant next to nothing. Something for other children to celebrate, for other people to enjoy. As for his life, it had always been a reminder of the ways in which he had very little in comparison with those. Not in a monetary sense. He hadn't cared about that so much, at least apart from being fed.

But in the sense of family.

While he'd had a long succession of uncles throughout the course of his childhood, it certainly wasn't the same as the sorts of families—whatever shape they took—who gathered around Christmas trees and dinner tables during that most festive season.

As an adult, it had meant little more to him than an excuse to throw themed parties at his clubs across the world. Everyone enjoyed the excuse to engage in revelry. All the better it was an excuse to cover up past pain and break-away issues with family, and lovers new and old.

He was under no illusion that many of the people who patronized his clubs were doing just that. But, it wasn't his job to worry about the emotional well-being of the people who danced their way to oblivion in his establish-ments on a nightly basis. He envied them their oblivion, in point of fact.

Typically, he felt nothing.

That sense of blurry freedom that came with alcohol and other substances didn't resonate with him. Not anymore. It violated his sense of control, and that was an unpleasant place for a man like himself to be in. He could not have what he wanted.

But then, that was true of a great many things lately. Astrid dominated his dreams, and now here it was, attending a Christmas tree lighting, on his wedding day. As the hol-iday held such little significance for him in general, this would be the marker for it for the rest of his life, whether he wanted it to be or not.

A marriage that wasn't a marriage. For a child who was no larger than an avocado at the moment.

But the child wouldn't stay the size of an avocado. Indeed, that child would grow. A son or daughter. One that he… He would have to hold it. Care for it. Granted, both he and Astrid could hire enough people to make sure that neither of them ever had to interact with their progeny if they chose. But he failed to see the point of that. It would make him barely a shade better than his father. And that just wasn't… It was a strange thing to him to discover he had standards, but it turned out he did.

A fact that was in ample evidence as he stood there in his bespoke tux, custom made for this day.

His wedding.

And tonight would be his wedding night. A wedding night that would herald the beginning of two years without sex. That was something he had not yet fought his bride on. There would be no way he would fall in line in such a way for that long. It simply wasn't reasonable, not for a man like him.

If nothing else, it was the principle of the thing. And he would not be dictated to.

"Two minutes."

The order from Astrid's petite, efficient little assistant came almost in defiance to that thought.

She was a pretty woman. With jet-black hair and golden-brown skin. Her glittering eyes and sharp features gave the impression of an astute field mouse, always in motion, and never missing even the faintest twitch of movement around her.

"Don't worry," he said, "I'm not going to leave your princess at the altar."

"I didn't think you were. Considering you were the one who pushed for this in the first place."

"I get the feeling you don't trust me."

She squared her shoulders. "I don't trust anyone. Not in the least."

"Interesting."

"Why?"

"You don't seem like the type of person who would be that hard."

"Very few of us are exactly what we seem. Astrid might be. Utterly and completely who she seems to be. And if you hurt her, I will have you executed."

"I have no plans to hurt your queen."

"Good. Then we have no problem."

She turned and left, and Mauro lingered for a moment, waiting until it was time for him to walk out of the holding room, as he thought of it, and toward the chapel. He was ushered to a back door that took him to the front of the sanctuary. All eyes were on them, and he knew that only approved photos were allowed. There were no cell phones present in the sanctuary. Only official photographers.

Thus was the royal protocol demanded by the very angry council that had been hands-off in every way in regards to the wedding, except for things like that. Things that made it all feel like a circus performance, more than anything else.

Not that he was opposed to a circus.

He was quite an accomplished ringmaster.

But he preferred to have greater control of the show. And not the kind being exerted here.

He took his position, and music began to play, a hush falling over the room. Neither of them had attendants. It was not a tradition in Bjornland, and anyway, it made no sense for him or for her. So it quickly became a bridal march, and the guests rose, turning toward the doors, which opened slowly, as if building anticipation for what they would reveal.

And what they did reveal was as a punch to his stomach.

She was exquisite. The first time he'd seen her she'd been in white, but she had been draped in fabric designed obviously to seduce. And he was a man who enjoyed the obvious. This was something more.

The lace gown clung to her curves, lovingly shaping to her beautiful body. The neckline was scalloped, the rounded curves drawing attention to breasts that he knew were soft and plump, and just the right size to fit in his hand.

She was like a goddess, her red hair cascading around her shoulders like a copper-gold halo, the light from behind seeming to ignite it. She did not have a veil, but rather a simple, jeweled circle that draped across her forehead.

She did not carry flowers. Her elegant hands were empty, her engagement ring glittering on her finger as she moved toward him, slowly, with purpose.

And suddenly, inspiration for just how he would handle his wife hit him, like a falling anvil.

She had used her body to bring them to this moment.

She had used him.

And he had absolutely no qualms now about using her. Until his desire for her was spent. Until his lust for her had been quenched. How long had she tormented him?

Months.

Months before he had found her again, and in the months since returning to Bjornland. Since their engagement. He had wanted her, and not allowed himself to have her. He had desired her, and not allowed himself to stake a claim.

Celibacy for two years? Why? When the most beautiful, intoxicating woman he'd ever had in his bed would be with him. Bound to him. When he would be living part-time in the palace of a necessity. He had easy access to her, and there was no reason he shouldn't make free use. At least, not in his estimation. There was terror in her eyes when she approached him, her hands trembling as she clasped his.

He wanted her to tremble before him. But for a different reason.

He wanted her out of her mind with need, as he had been. So incredibly naive. And he had not been naive.

He had never considered himself naive. But that was what she had done to him. And why shouldn't he reclaim himself?

He felt a slow smile cross his lips. And as the priest led them in their vows, he allowed himself to skim over the words. They didn't matter. Neither of them were forsaking all others for as long as they lived. There was no point to such a thing. Death would not be what parted them. But rather a calculated move on both their ends.

Love was not what had brought them together, so it did not matter what tore it asunder.

What mattered was tonight. Tonight, he would make his queen beg. Tonight, he would stake his claim in the marital bed.

She might not be his for life, but she was his for now. And he would make sure that the time they did have was spent naked.

That was what was wrong. Of course it was. Those moments when he felt compelled to understand her... They had never been about that. They had been replacement for what he truly desired. Her body, pressed against his. Her body, pliant and willing. His inside hers.

That thought got him through the ceremony, and then on to the reception.

And there was a moment, where the dance floor was cleared, and he and his bride were meant to dance together.

"Quite an elaborate party for a farce," he said the moment they were joined together, his voice nothing more than a husky whisper.

"What's the point of engaging in a farce if you don't go all the way?" Her spring-green eyes met his, and his gut tightened.

Indeed. There was no point engaging in a farce if it didn't go as far as it could. And that was what he intended to claim for himself tonight. All of it. Everything.

"The food is good," he said. "At least."

"What an odd detail to focus on."

"I also like your dress," he said, lowering his voice. "Or rather, I suspect that I like the body beneath it."

Her cheeks immediately turned pink. "Really? I mean… I don't know…why you would say that either. I would rather talk about the food."

"I like food a great deal," he said, very intentionally moving his hand so that it rested lower on her spine, hovering just above the curve of her ass. "You see, I spent a good deal of my childhood starving. And when you have experienced something like that… You become very protective of your next meal. And you appreciate it when you get it."

"That's terrible," she said, clearly uncomfortable. With the change in subject being so sudden, with everything.

"There's nothing to be sorry about. But you

see, this is why I enjoy the many vices I do. Because there were very few in my life as a child. Very little I could depend on. As I got older I learned to depend on myself. To make my own way. I have not been hungry since. It is a powerful thing, realizing you can change your own world."

Astrid nodded slowly. "I know. I know because that was what I had to learn. That I could change my world. That I could change my world and not violate my duty. Not the part of it that counted."

Something turned over inside him, and he felt a sense of grudging respect for her. And more than that... Understanding.

"We should be making our departure soon," he said.

"Should we?"

"A married couple very much in love is eager to escape on their wedding night. At least, that is my sense for it."

She looked away from him for a moment, and then back. "Right. I hadn't thought of that."

"Of course not," he said. "I did. In fact, I've

thought of little else beyond the fact that it's our wedding night since you stepped out in that dress."

Her eyes met his, wide and full of uncertainty. A strange thing with Astrid, who made it her business to at least appear certain at all times. "We have an agreement."

"Cannot agreements be amended?"

"You didn't give any indication that you wanted ours to be amended."

He was tired of talking. He was tired of being civil. This was the problem with business negotiations. It was the problem with needing to be civilized. At least when he had lived on the street there had been an honesty about it. About the transactions he'd engaged in with women who wanted his body, and would allow him to share their beds. In honesty and all motivation. It was clear. In the upper echelons of society, things like tact were required, and in Mauro's world those things were overrated.

He was done with words. He was done with verbal sparring.

He tightened his hold on her and she gasped, her head falling back, her eyes wide as she looked up at him. And he smiled. Because this reminded him of that night in the club. This reminded him why even if he could go back and undo what had happened between them knowing what he did now, he probably wouldn't.

He lowered his head, claiming her mouth with his. He parted her lips ruthlessly, sweeping his tongue in deep so that he could taste her. Taste this one thing between them that was utterly, completely honest.

They had an audience still. A captive one. They were out on the dance floor, and he was kissing her as if she were air and he was a man deprived of it. She clung to him, shaking, and that was when he knew he was going to get exactly what he wanted. Her, trembling beneath him. Begging for him.

He pulled away from her. "We should make our way to our room, don't you think?"

"Is that what this was about?" she said in a hushed whisper.

"No. You will find out exactly what this is about. When we go to your room." He thought for a moment that she might protest. But instead, she lowered her eyes, and then when she met his gaze again, they were blazing. "Then let's go to bed."

Her heart was racing, threatening to thunder out of her chest.

Yet, she had gone with him.

She had allowed him to lead her from the room. She was… She didn't know what was happening. He flew in the face of everything they had agreed, everything she had decided was appropriate. But he had kissed her, and then she didn't care. And then the idea of being married to him and not sharing his bed had seemed like an impossibility.

Because from the moment she had seen his picture for the first time in the papers, the idea of *not* being in his bed had been torture. She had been contending with that part of herself for the past few months.

Badly.

Because what did it say about her? That she was merely another groupie of his? One who had dressed up her motivations for being with him into something a bit more noble, when her reasoning was as base as anyone else's.

Right now, she felt base. Utterly and completely. Was reduced to a grasping creature made entirely of need and desire. That was all she was, it was all she could remember being. This woman who needed his touch more than she needed anything else.

That kiss the night they'd gotten engaged had been kerosene. And the kiss tonight had been a lit match against it. She was not strong. Not with him. Not with this.

She had stood tall and steady, with a will of iron since she had started to rule the country two years earlier. Before that she had been a model citizen. Studying, completing vast amounts of charity work. She had been strong. She had been for so very long.

She wanted something else now. She wanted to be held in someone else's strong arms. To let him hold on to her, and in so doing, take some of the weight of the crown, of her duty, off her. Even if it was just for a night.

How twisted was it that even her one and only time being with a man was rooted in a lie she told herself about it being all for her country?

When what it was had been… She had done it for her country. For herself. The baby part. But there had been other ways. But she had been willing to use him first. Before she resorted to science. Because at the end of the day she had wanted him. And it was all fine and good to try to make excuses, to try to tell herself she'd been selecting the finest specimen genetically.

She had told herself a lot of pretty lies.

What she had been was a girl with a crush. Latika had been right about that.

A girl who had a crush and no understanding of how to handle it.

She had spent a life dealing with people who catered to her too much, counterbalanced by constantly feeling opposed and undermined. Great authority, but with a very short leash. It made it difficult for her to figure out how to actually know people. How to relate to them.

The fact of the matter was she didn't know. And she never had. Her brother was her friend, but he was also a royal.

Latika was someone she also considered a friend, but Latika worked for her, and that created a strange sort of dynamic. She was isolated. And a bit spoiled. And she had behaved that way with him. Like a child entitled to something, one who had seen a shiny toy that she wanted, and had come up with all sorts of reasons why she deserved it.

But he wanted her now. And she wanted him. Even as remorse for her behavior flooded her, she still wanted him. Their rooms were next to each other. As was custom. He had not spent the night in the palace yet, and she wondered if he ever really would. But for appearances, they had readied the standard royal bedchambers. She wondered which room this would happen in. And what would happen after.

What would happen during.

The very thought made her shiver.

He dragged her down the empty corridor, and then suddenly pushed her up against the wall. His dark eyes blazed into hers, fearsome and filled with the dark emotion she couldn't name. It was like rage but hotter, desire but with a knife's edge.

He had not looked at her like this the night of the club. This was something more. Something deeper. Something that carried the layers that their relationship contained. A relationship she had forced him into.

Because he was here out of a sense of duty, she understood that all of a sudden. Not because he wanted to be her husband. Not because he was drawn to the idea of being married to a queen.

Not because he hungered for power or lusted for money.

Because of his own integrity.

She had convinced herself that she was acting with some kind of integrity when she had fooled him. But it had been self-serving.

Guilt lashed her like a whip. And for the first time she wondered if she was much more her father than she had ever previously imagined.

She had always thought of herself like her mother. And Latika had said, just tonight, that her mother would have approved of what she done.

But her mother had never harmed anyone. Would have never lied.

Her mother had told the truth when Gunnar and Astrid had been born. At great cost to herself in terms of her marriage.

Her mother believed in honesty, if not in showing love. It was her father who would have stooped to subterfuge to do what he had imagined he might have to do to save the kingdom.

Her actions were the same.

Right because she had found a loophole, because she imagined her own sense of justice to be the one true version of it.

And this was her penance. This man. This large, muscular angry man who was paying it right along with her.

She didn't know what he might do next. But he didn't make her wait long to find out.

He cupped her cheek, his touch gentle, and almost all the more terrifying for it. All that leashed strength. She could feel it. The force of his rage, and the way that he held it in check so that he could softly move his thumb over her cheekbone.

He lowered his hand then, gripping her hips tightly and surging forward, letting her feel the evidence of his desire. And then he lowered his head, kissing her, harder, deeper than he had back in the ballroom.

She was drowning in it. Drowning in him.

There was no more time for thought or self-flagellation. If this was her punishment she would submit to it. Because it was also her salvation.

Her moment.

Because he was strong. And he could hold her.

Because he was angry, and he could feel it in a thousand ways she had never really allowed herself to feel it.

Because he wanted her. It opened the door to allow her to feel her own want.

"Your room or mine?" he asked, his teeth scraping along the side of her neck. "Where shall I take you, out here in the hallway?"

The idea made her shiver with need, but she couldn't allow something like that. No.

"The bedroom," she said softly.

"As you wish."

He hauled her to him, lifting her off the ground and carrying her a few steps toward the bedroom, opening the door and propelling them both inside before he slammed it behind them. The room was familiar to her. She had inhabited it for the past couple of years. And yet, somehow with this man inside it, it felt completely different. He should look civilized in that custom-made tuxedo of his, the dark, elegant lines conforming gracefully to his body. But he didn't.

Instead, it seemed to provide a greater contrast to that strength, to his feral nature.

He tugged at his bow tie, letting it drape over his shoulders, and then he advanced on her, his movements quick and decisive as he grabbed hold of the zipper on the back of her dress and dragged it down, letting it fall to the floor, that custom creation that was worth thousands of dollars. He stepped over it as if it didn't matter and picked her up, carrying her to the large, ornate bed and placing her at the center of it, where she was surrounded by lush, velvet pillows, the cool, soft texture such a contrast to that hot, hard man above her.

"I would say that the night you approached

me in Italy was your show. Tonight it is mine, *cara mia*. And I will enjoy every moment of it."

He grabbed hold of his bow tie, tugging it from his shoulders, and then he took hold of her wrists, encircling them easily with one hand and drawing them up over her head. He smiled, then in one fluid motion took the strip of black fabric and tied it securely around her wrists, leaving her bound.

Desire and fear raced through her in equal measure, electricity shooting down between her thighs, the sensation of being hollow almost unbearable.

"Just making sure you stay where I want you."

"Mauro..."

"How badly do you want this?" he asked, tracing the edge of her lace bra cup with his fingertip. "How badly?"

"I need you," she whimpered.

"Well, let's see how long you can withstand this." He let his fingertips drip beneath the edge of the fabric, one calloused pad skimming her nipple, and she cried out.

"So sensitive," he said, chuckling darkly as

he pressed a kiss to that vulnerable place between her rib cage, down to her belly button, down farther. He pressed his mouth over her lace-covered mound, his breath hot against her skin as he scraped his teeth over the delicate fabric. She shivered, arching into him.

"That's the thing about going into a lion's den, *cara*," he said. "Sooner or later he's going to eat you."

He hooked his finger through the fabric on her panties and tugged it to the side, revealing her to his gaze. And then he moved in, laughing at her with bold, intense strokes. He curved his arms around her thighs, locking his fingers together and dragging her toward his face, holding her firmly against him as he continued to lavish attention on her with his lips, his tongue, his teeth.

He drove her to insane heights, and then brought her back from the edge. Over and over again until she was sobbing, crying with her need for release.

He traced circles around that sensitized bundle of nerves with his tongue, before lapping her in one slow lick, her climax pouring over her, leaving her spent and shaking and breathless.

But he wasn't finished. He began to toy with her, using his fingers, stroking her and teasing her until she found her release again. And again, this time with his mouth at her breast and his fingers buried deep inside her.

He brought her up to her knees, turned her away from him, where he lowered his head and laughed at her from a different angle, until she was trembling, begging for him to stop.

"Please," she said. "Finish."

"We are finished," he said, his voice rough. "I think you've had enough."

"You didn't… We didn't…"

"I said that was enough. It was a very long day."

He moved away from her, and she rolled onto her back, her hands still bound. He took hold of one end of the knot, freeing her in one easy tug that seemed to make a mockery of the way she had felt at his mercy.

Had she wanted to escape, she could have. The whole time.

The captivity had been only an illusion, and she had been so willing to sink into it because of what she wanted from him.

Because she had wanted him to hold her captive, to force her to feel those things, so that none of it was her responsibility.

He had proved that he could. But now... Now he was leaving.

"I'll see you tomorrow."

She was about to ask if he wanted her, if he had ever wanted her, but she could see the thick, hard outline of his erection pressed against the front of his black pants.

She could see that he wanted her, and he was still walking away.

"Good night," she said, the words thin and shaking.

"Good night."

And he didn't even have to get dressed to leave, because he was still fully clothed, and she was... Destroyed. Her bra was wrenched up over her breasts, but still clasped, her underwear shifted and torn in places.

She was humiliated. She had a feeling that he had intended to leave her humiliated.

She couldn't even feel angry, because she kept remembering the things that had occurred to her out in the hall. What she had done to him.

The humiliation he must've felt when she was on TV saying their child had no father.

Tonight he had demanded submission from her. He had exerted his control.

And now he was finished.

But she was not.

It took only a moment for Astrid to come to a decision.

She couldn't exist in this. In this world where he took his anger out on her body in such a way. She would give him an apology.

And she would make it one he would never forget.

Apologizing was another thing that Astrid had never done. But she was sure that she would do it well.

CHAPTER EIGHT

MAURO STRIPPED HIMSELF NAKED. He needed
a cold shower. Something. Anything to deal
with the desire that was still riding through
his body. He had intended to make her feel
out of control. To give her a taste of what she
had done to him that night at the club.

When she had pushed him past the point of
thinking clearly. Past the point of being sensible at all. And he had. He had, but in the
end, she had somehow still done something to
him. Overridden anything sensible. Destroyed
every barrier that he had placed between the
two of them.

The fact that he had been able to walk away
had been a damned miracle. And now...

He was shaking. He was. He had wanted to
make her tremble, had wanted to make her

boneless, mindless, and he had done it. But at what cost?

What cost to himself?

He did not know the man he was when he touched her.

He went up in flames.

The connecting door between their bedrooms suddenly opened, and he turned.

It was his wife.

And he was completely naked, so there was no hiding the fact that he was aroused, that his cock was hard, and ready for her. That he was in no way in control of his needs or desires.

"What are you doing here?"

She was still naked, her entire body bare and exposed to him, her pale curves temptation he was not sure he could fight. Was not certain he could overcome.

"I came because I owe you an apology."

She began to walk toward him, her hips swaying gently, her lush curves and wild, glorious hair, tumbled around her shoulders, making him think of an ancient goddess.

"You owe me an apology?" he asked, the words sounding stilted.

"Yes. I owe you a great many things. And one evening will not be sufficient in making amends. But I would like to try."

"What are you doing?"

She moved nearer to him, pressing her palm against his chest, her touch soft, bewitching. "If you have to ask, then I'm not doing a very good job."

She walked a circle around him, slowly, appraising his body, her fingertips grazing lightly over his skin as she did. She stopped in front of him, those green eyes intent on his, blazing.

"I am a queen," she said. "I have been, my entire life, even before I bore the title. That's how it works. When you are the heir, you must behave as if you are from the beginning. There is no other option. There will be no quarter given. And I have… I have lived my life that way. Above reproach in many ways, as we discussed. But also without nuance. Without subtlety. There is no humility in me. I didn't learn it. I like to think there's compassion. Caring. And that mostly in my life I have acted in a way that would not do harm to others. But

I have always been set apart, and I have always lived that way. My connections with those around me… I'm incapable of separating them from my status. I am not like you."

"Indeed," he said, grabbing hold of her wrist and holding her fast. "Because I'm not blue-blooded like you?"

"Yes," she whispered. "Yes."

Rage fired through him, but it wasn't because of that. It was because of all of the feelings inside him. The deep, roaring desire that he had to take her now, in spite of the fact that he had told himself he would not.

"You've lived more than one life," she continued. "And because of that I think you understand more. I think you see more. I have my struggles. Things that I have had to overcome. But they are in this world. My battlefield has been an ivory tower. I see my country from an elevated stance. My people. It is a necessity in many ways so that I can have an overview. So that I can know as much, and have time to look at it all. I fear sometimes that leads me to see people in general as statistics. Or chess pieces. I saw you as a chess piece. And I used you and for that I owe you an apology." She looked up at him again, and desire made his gut tighten.

"I am a queen," she repeated. "And I bow to no man. I never have. But for you... For you I will get on my knees."

And without warning she did just that, her red hair sliding over her shoulders as she went down. And then, she looked back up at him as she raised her hand, wrapping it around his hardened length.

And he knew he was lost. Knew that there was no way he could fight this. Not now.

He was finished. His control was at an end. And when that slick, pink tongue darted out over his arousal, when she closed her lips over him and took him in deep, there was no more thought.

She clung to him as she lavished attention on his body with that imperious mouth.

He had heard it issued demands, had heard it whisper lies. And now that same, traitorous tongue slid effortlessly over him and stoked the flame of desire in his stomach.

Women had done this for him many times.

It was not an unusual act, but there was something in the way she did it that made it something entirely new. Because she was queen. Because she was Astrid.

Because she made him feel the way no woman ever had before.

Because. Because many things he didn't want to think about. Didn't want to acknowledge.

He was at the verge of being able to hold back no more. And he didn't want that. Didn't want it to end that way. Not now.

"Enough," he growled, pulling her away from him.

"I haven't finished," she said, a small smile tilting her lips upward.

"If you wish to truly bow before me, my Queen, if you truly wish to make amends, and allow me use of your royal body, then I have a decidedly better way for you to kneel."

He swept her up off the floor and into his arms, carrying her over to the bed and positioning her there, on her hands and knees, her deliciously shaped ass on full display for his enjoyment.

He stroked himself, looking at her, at the image that she created there.

He was a fool. An absolute fool. He should have turned away from this long ago, but now it was too late. Now, he had to have her. Now, there was no going back.

If she wanted to apologize for her treachery, then he would take it out on her body. It would be no hardship. She was giving herself to him freely, and it was because of the ruthless seduction he had subjected her to only moments before.

This was control.

He still had control.

He pressed his fingers between her legs, pushing inside her tight, wet body as he tested her readiness.

She was ready. So very ready, and so desirous of him that it nearly made him lose his control then and there.

He joined her on the bed, positioning himself at her entrance and pushing inside slowly. She was so tight, so impossibly perfect.

She moaned, slow and long as he withdrew and thrust back home. And as he pounded inside her, he watched. The way that her elegant spine arched as she felt her pleasure build, the way she curled her fingers around the bed-spread.

He couldn't see her face, but there was no denying it was her. His queen.

On her knees for him.

He held on to her hips, showing no mercy as he pushed them both toward a release he knew would consume them both.

And as his pleasure roared through his blood, screamed through his system like a freight train, there was one last thought be-fore his release burned each and every one away like stubble and hay beneath the flame.

She was on her knees for him.

But he was on his knees too.

And then there was nothing. Oblivion. Sweet, desperate need being satisfied as he poured himself inside her.

His queen. His wife.

When it was through, she collapsed onto her stomach on the bed, then rolled to her side, curling up into a ball, her expression sleepy and satisfied.

And he remembered the way she had run out on him the first night.

How he had tried to run out on her not long ago.

It would be better to keep her with him. To keep her here.

He had tried it the other way, and he didn't like it.

If this was to be about him staking his claim and finding his place, then he was free to make that decision.

And so he wrapped his arm around her waist and drew her up against him, holding her tight.

He was on the verge of deciding on an entirely new plan.

One where Astrid being his wife meant her spending her nights in his bed. And only his.

For there was no way he would ever allow another man to touch her, he realized that now.

She was his woman. And she was carrying his child.

And the decision to hold her all night seemed to make everything clear.

His.

Only his.

CHAPTER NINE

OF ALL THE things Astrid expected to wake to the morning after her wedding, a scandal wasn't one of them.

After all, there had been ample opportunity for a scandal to break over the past couple of weeks, and yet none had.

But then, Bjornland being isolated as it was, it was often cloistered from the rest of the world, with news filtering out slowly. But, given that Mauro was arguably more famous than she the world over, she would have expected something like this to break sooner.

The breakfast table was covered in newspapers. And she didn't have to be terribly insightful to figure out that someone from her father's council was responsible for the delivery of the day's tidings.

"What is this?" Mauro asked, taking his seat at the table with utter confidence.

He did everything with supreme confidence. As he had shown her last night. Repeatedly. Until he had made her shake. Made her scream. Until she could no longer tell where her body ended and his began.

Something had changed between them last night. What had started in anger had ended with something else. It wasn't absent anger. It was imbued with an intensity that spoke of nearly every emotion.

All she knew was that by the time it was all over, the most natural thing in the world had been to curl up against him.

In many ways, she felt like a lamb choosing to sleep nestled up against the side of a lion. Mostly, she just had to trust that he wasn't going to eat her.

She had the feeling that Mauro was undecided as yet.

"Our reckoning," Astrid said, lifting one of the papers up. "At least, that's what it appears to be."

"I see my past has caught up with me."

Astrid began to read past the inflammatory headline.

The brand-new consort to the queen of Bjornland used to work as a rent boy.

There was no real escaping from the truth inherent in the headline. There were some seedy details included. Though, it didn't sound as if Mauro had been working the street so much as being passed around among bored older women.

"Why didn't you tell me?" she asked. "More interestingly, why has this not been in the press before?"

"Because, one of the women would have had to be willing to admit the fact that they paid me for sex. And apparently Lady Catherine is just close enough to death's door to do such a thing now." Astrid continued to stare at him, trying to figure out what he was feeling. He didn't look upset, nor did he look ashamed.

Being connected to such a scandal was the stuff of nightmares for her, and it made her skin feel like it was too tight for her body. Mauro was simply… He didn't seem to feel a thing at all.

"Also," he continued. "I make my living from scandal, Astrid. My clubs are all about debauchery. At what point do you suppose this would have been an interesting headline for a man famous for immoral acts? No, it's only interesting now."

She pressed her fingers to the center of her forehead. "This is a fantastic look to show the world," she said.

"You chose me as the father of your child."

"And now these are things our child will see. It's printed in black-and-white..."

"Do you have regrets, my Queen?"

The words were so cold and hard, and they hit her square in the chest. "No. Not in the way that you mean. But there are consequences for this. For our son or daughter. That's what I care about."

"Not about your own pristine reputation?"

She took in a labored breath. "I would be lying to you if I said I didn't care at all for the reputation of my country, and myself. But I can't deny my own involvement in bringing myself here. Is there anything else that you need to tell me?"

"I came from the gutter, Astrid. You do not ascend to success in the amount of time I did without crossing a few barriers between one side of the law and the other. Without making bargains with morality. You simply don't. I regret nothing of what I did, because it brought me to where I am. Once I figured out that I could control my fate, I took every opportunity to do so. At a certain age I discovered that women quite enjoyed me. And if it was something I was going to go out and do anyway for recreation, why not get a place to stay for the night, a hot meal. And some cash in my pocket. I have no moral qualms about what I did."

For the first time, she saw a spark in his face. In his eyes. "The rest of the world does," he continued, stabbing a headline with his forefinger. "The rest of the world that leaves people behind, blames them for accidents of birth that see them thrust into a guaranteed lifetime of poverty. And believe me, we will be able to overcome this. Were I a woman in the same position... I fear my reputation would be beyond salvation. Fortunately, I'm a man, and one that now has money."

"Is that what you think?"

"It's what I know. My mother was nothing but a whore in the eyes of the world until the day she died. No one ever admitted her to their parties. Not even with me as her son. Of course, by the time of her death I wasn't quite as well-known as I am now. I imagine at a certain point any amount of money can erase a life of harlotry. My mother did what she had to. For us. Because my father, though he possessed the ability to support us, decided to pretend we didn't exist. No, don't ask me to apologize for selling what I had. Anymore than she should apologize for it. People with money are willing to buy it, and they're willing to pay quite a bit. They would rather buy sex than buy dinner for anyone in the slums, so you tell me what's to be done."

"I didn't say I was judging you," she said, but at the same time, she felt like something had shifted. Because what had happened between them last night was not a simple transaction. Then she wondered if it was for him.

It was deep and elemental and intimate. Had been from the first time. She couldn't imagine simply handing her body over for a few dollars and a place to sleep.

Because you've never been asked to do it. You've never had to. You were protected and you were insulated, and the most despicable thing you ever had to put up with was your father not believing in you.

She gritted her teeth. "How long did you do that?"

"Truthfully? Not even quite a year. Just something I did to save up money and move myself on to the next thing. I did that. I also worked as a bouncer at a club. That's where I got familiar with that sort of environment."

"Did you... Did it bother you? To be with women you didn't want?"

"I could make myself want them all. And if I didn't want them specifically, I could make myself do it for the money. A soft bed is quite arousing when the alternative is the streets."

She blinked, ignoring the scratchy feeling behind her eyes. "What did your mother think?"

"We never discussed it," he said, chuckling darkly. "Clearly. But then, she always behaved as if I might not know what she did with men coming through the house at all hours."

"So, you had a house?"

"Yes. For a time. I left when I was sixteen, because I couldn't bear it anymore. To watch her submit herself to that. Neither could I tolerate the ones who came to my room after, seeing if I would give for free what my mother had charged for. Don't worry. No one ever did anything to me. I was lucky. And that's the other thing, in the grand scheme of things, given my background, I was quite lucky. What I did, I did with a certain amount of choice involved. It's more than I can say for many like me. Don't waste any sympathy on me."

"I have sympathy for the headlines."

"They don't bother me. Though, I wonder if I should be concerned about you."

"There need be no concern," she said, pushing herself into a standing position.

She despised the weakness that had settled into her limbs. Hated that the press had been able to make her feel this way. That her father's councilmen were succeeding in trying to sabotage them so soon after the wedding.

This idea that bad press should be avoided at all cost, that being scandal free was an essential, was old thinking. Old thinking that was part of the Astrid she'd been before. Before she'd decided to take control of her own life by having her own child.

That Astrid could not care so much for scandal.

That Astrid would do things differently.

She took a breath. "I will be damned if anyone is allowed to write the story but us. We have done our best to control it from the beginning, and I don't see why we can't continue on as we began. We should go. We should go to Italy, visit your clubs. Show that I am in absolute support of you and all that you are."

He arched a brow. "Are you sure you don't just want to have a press release where you stand behind me looking regretful while I confess my many sins?"

She waved a hand. "No. I have no interest in that. None at all."

"Reputation is of no concern to me," he said.

"Well, it is of a concern to me," she said. "And I will not allow the press to decide what that reputation is. I'm clearing my schedule."

"Shall we take your private plane or mine?" he asked.

"We both have private planes?"

"Yes indeed," he said.

"Well, that just borders on absurd."

"It might, but I think it would be difficult for us to consolidate, given our busy schedules."

"I suppose."

"Mine, then," he said. "It has the whiskey I like on board."

"That isn't fair. I can't drink any."

"I never said any of this was going to be fair."

Astrid frowned. "I don't suppose you did."

The doors to the dining room burst open, and in charged one of the men from the council, his face red. "Do you see the censure you have opened us up to?" he railed against Astrid. "If your father were alive to see the disgrace that you have brought on his country…"

Mauro stood, slowly and decisively, his manner intimidating, his body radiating with a dark energy. "If your father were alive, he would see a woman standing strong in the face of embarrassingly tiny adversaries. And that is what you will continue to see in the coming days. I never met the old king, so I cannot speak confidently of what would give him pride. But he would at least not be able to deny the strength and sense of honor that Queen Astrid exudes."

Astrid said nothing, she simply watched as the councilman turned and walked out of the room, clearly not at all mollified by Mauro's interference, but likely gone off to lick his wounds, as he clearly didn't possess the wherewithal to stand against a man of Mauro's presence.

She could have defended herself. She had done it for years now. This was hardly going to be the straw that broke the camel's back. But she was tired, and she was reeling from the revelations in the paper in front of her.

And for all that Mauro was tangled up in the challenges she was dealing with now, she was grateful to have had him there to stand with her. It wasn't always about needing to be rescued or defended. But sometimes it was good to know that someone was there to stand with you. To be the first to speak in defense.

To know that someone else was on your side.

She didn't know when that switch had occurred. Mauro had felt like yet another in a line of adversaries, and suddenly now she felt as if they had melded into a team. If nothing else, Mauro would want a stable environment for their child.

She took a breath. "I think we have a plane to catch."

By the time the plane touched down in Italy, yet another scandal had broken.

Mauro was ready to track down journalists and cockroaches from his past and present alike and create some real scandal.

He minded the rumors about his life as a prostitute less than the stories that greeted them the moment they touched down in his homeland.

His father had come forward.

Dominic Farenzi, titled old duke and part of

one of Italy's oldest aristocratic families, had finally claimed his son.

Oh, not for a happy reunion, no, the duke would never do such a thing. He wanted his name in the press. To attach himself to the scandal by dragging Mauro's name down further.

And, of course, it made perfect sense. Mauro had taken a different last name as he had ascended the ranks, partly because he didn't want every old relative of his mother's coming out of the woodwork to demand endless paydays. He had wanted to avoid situations that involved blackmail.

His former clients—the women he slept with—would have most certainly recognized him, but Dominic would have no reason to recognize him on sight. They had met only once, and Mauro had been young.

He had looked up at the old man with all of the hope only a boy could still possess after such a miserable upbringing—and the old man had gazed back with a sneer. And told Mauro exactly what he was. Not a part of that lineage, but a mistake. A mistake that should have been nothing more than a stain on his sheets.

But now… Now that his profile had been raised, and now that he was royalty by marriage, his father had made the connection, and more than that, had seen his opportunity to use the connection. Money… The old man had that. This was something more, and obviously he wished to use it.

"So, you're not a commoner," Astrid said when they were settled into his awaiting sports car and driving through the winding streets.

"I might as well be. I'm a bastard. Dukes and bastards are a time-honored tradition, in every culture, I should think. I am not royalty. Not by any real standard. But there are any number of people clearly willing to use this connection, and I would have told you he would be the last person to do it, out of a sense of self-preservation. But I suppose this is the problem with aging enemies. They figure perhaps they only have a certain number of years to even concern themselves with answering for the consequences of their actions. Why not see what happens?"

"All fine for him. But he's playing with your life."

"Though, in this case there is nothing for me to be ashamed of. Though I would suppose that vicious commentary about my mother will follow. Thankfully, she's dead. And none of this will be her problem."

"I'm sorry," she said. "I had no idea... When I chose you I miscalculated in more ways than I realized."

"I imagine you didn't wish to choose the bastard son of a twisted old man who also moonlighted as a gigolo to be the father of your baby."

"That's not what I meant," she said quickly. "I only meant that I didn't know how much the media would be able to discover. And how much they would use against you. They can be brutal and vicious, my mother instructed me on that early on."

"It doesn't affect me much," he said. "I have been brutal and vicious to myself in the public sphere for years. I found self-deprecation to be the best defense. But, it's not exactly a good look for the queen of a nation I don't suppose."

"Possibly not," she said.

"Did you always know who your father was?"

"I can't remember exactly when I truly became aware of who he was and what that meant. Yes. It was never a secret. Not for me. I think my mother wanted me to be aware. I think she wanted me to know that there was a certain amount of injustice at play. She wanted me to understand. Something that I appreciate greatly. Because it helped to shape me into what I was. It helped me understand where power came from. There are titles. And then there is money. And both bring their own kind of power. It's certainly better to have them together. One can be earned, and one cannot be. I decided never to waste my time caring about something that I could never go out and earn for myself. And so, I simply decided to work at getting money. Because I would be damned if the last word on who I was came from a man who didn't care whether or not I lived or died."

"I understand," she said. "I mean, I really understand now why you won't abandon your child. Why it means something to you. I'm sorry. It was so… I was only thinking of myself and my goals. Sometimes I get so focused on this idea of the greater good, and I remove the humanity from it. In this case, I decided that the greater good was something that I wanted. And I truly didn't think of you."

"It doesn't matter. What matters is that I won't be like my father. Ever."

"I believe it." She looked out the window, at the buildings that closed in around them, tall and brick, rebelling against the age that was beginning to crack at the foundation.

The farther on they went, the more faded the glory of the buildings around them. It did not appear that they were headed in a direction where Mauro would live, or have a club.

"Where are we going?"

He was questioning that himself. Questioning it because he had decided that he would take her to see, so that she had the whole story, but it was one thing to think it, and quite another to do it. He imagined that Astrid had never been near a slum in her life.

"It's the whole story. So that there are no more surprises. I think that is important to see."

Astrid was quiet after that, and he maneuvered the sleek car around the corner, until they reached a sparse, wasteland of an area that contained a crumbling apartment building, and tarp set up as tents around the property.

"If you're lucky, you live in there," he said.

"Oh," she said, her eyes wide as she took in the sprawl of humanity around them. "This is where you're from?"

"Yes." He cleared his throat. "I imagine you have not had an exposure to such things."

"No, I have. I've been involved in quite a few outreaches worldwide where I went and distributed medical supplies and food. But... It's not the same as living in it. It's not the same as... Growing up this way."

"This is what I am. I have no shame in it, and I never have. The press is going to attempt to make it a shameful thing, and I'm sure that there are only more lurid details of my sexual exploits to come. There will likely be women who spent wild nights with me in my club eager to tell their story. For all I know, more of my… Clients from my early years. These things will continue to happen. As long as there is money or fame to be extorted, it will occur. It was one thing when I was selling sin. It's quite another in this position."

"It's all right," she said. "I… I did this to escape from the hold that the men on my father's council had over me. I did this to gain independence. What good is independence if I'm still held hostage by a desperate need to make myself look better than I actually am? My desperate need to be something I'm not. Whatever the true nature of our relationship is… We are having a baby."

There was one last place. His house, if it still stood.

"Just a little bit farther," he said.

Their home was at the wall of a dead end, beneath an office building that he had never imagined housed businesses that were terribly legitimate. The place looked abandoned now, the windows boarded up, a notice posted on the side.

"This is where we lived," he said.

"This is your house?"

"Yes."

"Where does your father live?"

He turned toward the vast mountain that rose up above the buildings around them.

"There. He lives there. And he has a view of the whole city, down to the slums. While we had a view of those mansions up on the hill. And I knew that the man who fathered me was there. Somewhere. That he was there looking down on that very house, this very spot, and feeling nothing. It was motivating. And I…"

He parked the car suddenly and got out, looking around to make sure there was no one loitering nearby.

He had no doubt that he was well able to handle any attacker who might come out from behind the shadows. He had learned to defend himself against grown men when he was just a boy. Maturity, and years of hard labor in the gym, had only honed his physique further.

Plus, he was ruthless. He had learned to fight, not in arenas, but in situations that could very well have turned into life or death. That meant when he was under threat, he gave no quarter.

And should anyone step forward to threaten Astrid—to threaten his child—he would not hesitate to do what needed to be done. He took a breath of the air, stale down here, and warmer, boxed in by these tall, narrow buildings. And it reminded him of what it meant to be a boy. To be trapped here.

To be helpless.

He loosened his tie, feeling as if he was choking on the air around them.

He felt a hand on his shoulder and turned to see Astrid standing there. "Are you all right?"

"I'm fine. I haven't been back here, not since I left my mother's home. After that I went off to find my way, and once I had acquired enough, I sent for her. I bought her a house. One up there on the hill. So that she could look down on everything here, the same as he had done all those years. So much hard living. She did not last long after. I blame him. I always will."

"I don't blame you."

"I met him once. My mother told me which

house was his, and I climbed the hill. I walked right up to that house, and I stood there on the front porch, full of the bravado of a young boy, just barely more than thirteen. Convinced I was a man. I knocked on the door, and I asked to see him. I thought they were going to send me away, but he heard me. He heard me and he came to the door. I thought that if I explained to him what our situation was… What my mother was forced to do…" That moment, that sick humiliation and shame, that deep, unmet need all seemed close to the surface now, rolling through his stomach like an angry ball of fire.

"He knew. And what's more, he made it very clear to me that my mother had not turned to prostitution as a desperate single mother. But rather, that was how she had found him."

"How vile," Astrid said. "How could he speak to you like that?"

"Oh, he took great joy in it. In making sure that I knew that I was never going to be seen the way that he saw my half brothers and sisters. That my mother's blood made me unsuitable. But you know… It's his. It's his blood that

I regret the most, not the blood of the woman who did what she had to, to allow us both to survive. Who cared for me, even when it was hard. No, I don't feel shame over carrying her blood. But when I think too deeply of his, I can feel my skin crawl. After that, I decided I would never covet what I could not have, not again. I took great pains to make sure that I could have whatever it was I pleased. I started making plans. I thought about all the places people went when they had money, and I figured that what I would want was a way to take the money of those people. Which is what I've done. Hotels. Clubs. Resorts and destination vacation spots. I appeal to those who have money to invest in fantasy. And with that I've built something real. With that, I will make a life for my child far and away what my mother was able to do for me, in spite of how hard she tried."

"Your father is a disgusting, opportunistic animal. We will give him no satisfaction with what he's trying to do."

"Oh, the press will give him plenty, I have no concerns about that."

"How unfair," she said. "How unfair that they all want to give you attention now."

"Let them," he said. "It makes no difference to me. It only proves that suddenly I have something that they want. Now my father can use me. How novel. All those years I could have used him. Well, fortunes of change."

He stepped away from the old house. From the tightness in his chest.

"I shall take you to my offices."

"Oh, really?"

"Yes," he said decisively. "I have spent a great deal of time in your domain, my Queen. It's time you came to mine."

CHAPTER TEN

MAURO'S OFFICES WERE impressive indeed. The contrast of the brilliant, steel-and-glass-framed building when juxtaposed against the slums they had just visited struck Astrid particularly hard as he ushered her into his office, paneless glass windows making up the entirety of the walls, overlooking Rome. Overlooking even the houses on the hills.

And she understood it. What it meant. Why it mattered. She understood what had shaped him.

And she felt...

It was a strange thing, to have this man let her in that way. She couldn't say that she knew very many people in such a deep way that she did him.

She knew no one in such an intimate fashion.

But his showing her the slums… The house. Talking about his father.

It was all new. This feeling for another person. This feeling like she knew him. Like she could feel the things he felt.

He pressed his hand to her lower back as he led her deeper into his office, and somehow as he did that, she felt as if he had wrapped his hand around her heart and squeezed it tight.

"These are the corporate offices. As you can see, I have a few."

"Yes. You do." It wasn't just a stark contrast to the slums, but to the palace and Bjornland, which was gilded and old-fashioned in every way. "The clutter of the palace must drive you crazy," she observed.

"I was thinking the same about you," he said. "You enjoy that restaurant we went to the night we got engaged. And it's quite spare. You also seem particularly fond of the ring I bought you."

She squeezed her hand into a fist, feeling embarrassed that he had seen through her so easily. "It is very pretty. Yes, I suppose the rooms in the palace are not necessarily to my taste."

"You should have them redone."

"That's simple?"

"Why not?"

"Because of tradition, and things. It's hardly... It's hardly appropriate to go changing everything right when you're crowned."

"Is it not?" he asked.

"I wouldn't think."

"You've been queen for two years."

"Yes," she agreed. "I have been."

"If you're not afraid to take control of your own destiny, you should be able to take control of your bedroom decor."

"Fair enough," she replied. "Perhaps I will do a bit of a redesign when we get back." She frowned. "If we... Are you coming back with me?"

It was such a vulnerable statement. So very silly. She didn't know why she was exposing herself to potential rejection like that. Especially considering he wasn't supposed to matter. But then, he wasn't supposed to have revealed such intimate and crushing things about himself either. He wasn't supposed to be human. That was the crux of the problem. The longer she was around this beautiful, god of a man, the more she saw his humanity. And that was dangerous in a particular way nothing else had ever been.

"I will be back intermittently," he said.

"I see."

"Though, I should make one thing very clear," he said.

"What is that?"

"That the idea that you might spend time in other men's beds is now off the table."

"Is it?" She tried to sound surprised, or maybe even mildly annoyed about his heavy-handed proclamation, but instead, she was certain that some of her hopefulness had broken through.

"After what happened on our wedding night… I should think that was quite obvious."

"What happened?"

"The explosion between us."

"It is as it ever was," she said, trying to sound casual. "Is it different than the first time? Is it different than it normally is?"

Of course, that last question revealed just how much she didn't know.

"It is never like that. Not with anyone else. And if you cannot feel how it was different than our first time…"

"I do," she said.

"Then surely you must know that this is a fact. There will be no one else."

"What about for you?"

"I don't want anyone else."

"And if you did?"

"I suspect we would have a discussion about it before anything occurred. I am nothing if not honest."

"So, should I wish to sleep with another man, we will have a discussion?"

"There will be no discussion. I would separate the man's head from his body."

"Well, that doesn't seem equitable."

"I didn't say that it was."

"I'm a queen," she said. "The rightful queen of Bjornland. You marrying me does not make you a king."

"But we are in my kingdom now," he said, a smile spreading slowly across his chiseled face. "And that is one reason I took you to see the slums that I grew up in. So you would understand. You think that you know because you have read articles. You think that you know because you have spent time in my bed. But unless you have seen where I was. You will not understand what it means that I am here."

So, he hadn't been showing her out of any desire to connect with her emotionally. She didn't know why, but that made her feel… She didn't like it. She wanted something more from him, and she hated that she did. She wanted something more from him, and the very idea of it made her feel uncomfortable. And also needy and vulnerable in ways that she didn't want to confront.

"I'm very impressed," she returned.

"I don't require that you be impressed. But you should understand. I am a man who sees no obstacle that he cannot overcome. If you think that you might win with me, *cara*, you are sadly mistaken."

The feelings that rolled through her body were tumultuous. She had no idea how to parse them all. On the one hand, his stubbornness, the fact that he was not intimidated at all by who she was, made her feel like she was adrift. She was accustomed to subtle challenges, not open ones. It also made her feel alive. Alive and particularly invigorated. That she could step into this place that was his, only his, as she had done that first night, and to be consumed by his world. By him. Even if only for a moment.

She wished that she could spend more time with him here. And maybe she would. There was no reason she couldn't split her time between Bjornland and Italy. Her ability to govern was not impacted by whether or not she was directly in residence in the palace.

But he hadn't said that he wanted her to. Instead, he had simply said that he would be staying here.

"There is a gala tonight," he said suddenly.

"Oh?"

"Not the sort of thing I usually bother myself with. In fact, I usually take great joy in turning down the invitations."

"All right."

"But we are in a different position now, are we not?"

"You are," she said. "I attend galas the world over, as a representative of my country."

"And I tend to sink deeper into debauchery at my clubs."

"We make choices."

"Well, now I'm going to make a different one. As we are making a show of solidarity, I figure there will be no better way of doing that than appearing so grandly upon the world stage."

"I suppose so," she returned.

"You are mine," he said. "And the world has only understood thus far, I think, that I might be yours. But they will understand after to-night."

She was his? But how did he mean that? And why did she want it to mean…? Why did she want it to have meaning?

The way he made her feel when they were alone in the dark was a heady, sensual rush that affected not just her body but also her soul.

It had nothing to do with performance and everything to do with… She didn't know.

She didn't know, and she hated not knowing. "That sounds ominous," she said, instead of any of the things she'd been thinking.

His dark eyes caught and held hers, and didn't let go. "You will understand too. After tonight. You will understand."

Mauro was not one to question his own decision-making. He never had been. There had never been time for any such things. He was a man of action, by necessity. He had never been one to Monday morning quarterback the decisions he'd made to propel his life in the direction that he wanted it. He was questioning himself now. If only a bit.

He was a headline the world over at the moment, and while in many ways he didn't mind at all, in others…

But he was set to beard the lion tonight.

His father would be at this event. That was one of the many reasons he had avoided things like this in the past, as much as he tried to pretend otherwise. He had allowed his father's presence to deter him from joining society in Italy for a number of years.

He had always told himself it was because there was no point.

He was not a man who dealt in galas, after all.

He liked to appeal to the darker, more sensual side of the moneyed set in the world. Liked to gather in the blackness, carrying out sultry, libidinous acts in the shadows.

He was going to have to work at changing the headlines. Not for himself, not even for Astrid, but for his child.

He did not deserve to see his father only as a horror, who was also the son of one.

He might not feel shame over what he was, but his child invariably would. And that would have to change.

He straightened the cuffs on his jacket and looked toward the room in his penthouse that Astrid had secreted herself in earlier. He had forced the issue of being the one to choose her gown, and she had been put out with him, as she had a stylist who was in charge of selecting all of the dresses she wore for public appearance.

Mauro had made the point—the excellent

point, if he said so himself—that Astrid appearing in something a bit different would only support the narrative about their relationship being a defining one.

The gown he had chosen, with the help of his assistant, was exactly what he wished to see his beautiful, curvy wife in, but now she seemed to be hiding out.

"Astrid," he said. "We are about to pass the point of being fashionably late."

The door cracked slightly. "Do you care?"

"No. I like being fashionably late, because it makes people talk. But I thought you might care."

"I don't think I can possibly go out in this."

"It is nothing compared to that white dress you wore the night you first seduced me."

"That was different," she said archly. "I was not being photographed, and I was trying to seduce you."

"And tonight you are my wife. And we are in my part of the world, and I expect for you to present yourself in such a manner. I will wear any ceremonial dress that you require in your country. But you must indulge me here."

"Okay. So that is how it will work when we are in Italy, or when we are in Bjornland. But what about when we're in… Holland?"

"We will both wear wooden shoes. Now, show me the dress."

She opened the door all the way, and the tiger that he was barely keeping leashed inside him leaped forward.

He no longer wanted to go out. Rather, he wanted to spend the entire evening exploring the ways in which that gown clung to her body.

It was a burnished gold that set off a fire in her glossy red hair, the color picking up gold tones in that pale skin of hers, as well. It glimmered as it clung to each and every curve, the neckline a deep V that accentuated her lush body.

"It is a bit much," she said, breezing past him and moving to where her makeup bag was. She produced a tube of red lipstick, and applied it to her mouth, making her look even more of a siren than she had a moment before.

He brought her up against his side, and guided her toward the door, her figure fitting more perfectly against his than he ever could've imagined.

"When we come home," he murmured, as they got into the elevator, "I greatly look forward to stripping this dress off you."

"What exactly are we doing?" she asked.

"What do you mean? Right now, we are going to a gala."

"I mean… What are we doing? In private. Behind closed doors. Where we have no reason to be putting on a show. What are we doing? Because it was one thing when we had an arrangement, for the benefit of our son or daughter. It was one thing when we were putting on a show for the media. But this idea that we will spend our nights together… As if it's just an assumed thing… I don't understand the purpose of that."

He said nothing as they walked through the lobby of the spectacular apartment building he called his own. They were ushered into a limousine, and he took his seat right beside her, pressing his hand over the top of her small, soft one.

"I don't understand why we wouldn't burn

out any chemistry that exists between us. People are so prudish about sex and attraction, but it's something that's never made much sense to me."

"I don't suppose it would. You used it as a commodity when you were young, but I did not. For me, it is about connection in some way, at the very least. It is inescapable as far as I'm concerned. I do not know of another way to see it. And I don't wish to put us in the position where things would become acrimonious between us should you decide... Should you decide that you feel an attraction for another woman. And what will happen when we decide to separate? What then? As I see it, it can only go two ways. We must decide that it is temporary, and that we are business partners. Or we must decide it's forever."

Forever.

He had never thought of anything in those terms before. Mostly because he didn't think very many steps ahead. He saw his goal, and he achieved it. And then he went on to the next. He enjoyed the excesses that he had at his disposal at any given time, with great relish. And he did nothing to concern himself with heavy things, things that pertained to the future. And she was asking him to choose. Nothing or forever.

He was a man who had no issue being decisive. And yet, he found this was one question he could not answer with an instantaneous snap of his finger.

Just another way in which this little queen confounded him.

The car rolled up to the front of the beautiful, historic hotel that the gala was being held in. The white marble shone pale in the moonlight, a beacon of all that he had ever aspired to as a boy.

And beside him there was Astrid.

A woman of pale marble, who wasn't cold to the touch, but warm and so very alive. So very enticing.

"We will speak more after the gala."

"We will speak," she said insistently. "I won't have you drowning out my common sense with your temptation."

Temptation. He would happily show her some temptation, and give her a very solid display on why they did not need to make such a definitive bargain between them.

He took hold of her hand, and pulled her forward, wrapping his arms around her and bringing her up onto his lap, so that she could feel the hardness and intensity that only she seemed to be able to create in him. And he kissed her. Not a slow tasting, but a fierce claiming. A promise. Of everything he was going to use to convince her that this heat between them needed to be thoroughly explored, and there would be no rationalizing that away on her part.

After all, she was the one who had ignited this need inside him. All of this was her fault. And her daring to try and put up a barrier between them now was something he could not let stand.

He cupped her face, taking the kiss deep, sliding his tongue against hers until he drew a fractured moan from her body. And then he pulled away.

"Yes," he said. "We will resume this discussion after the gala."

He opened the door to the limo, brushing

past the driver, who was attempting to hold the door for them, and instead, held it open for Astrid before taking her arm and closing it behind them.

"You shouldn't try to do the poor man's job for him," Astrid said, clearly attempting to sound as healthy as possible and to seem un-affected by the kiss they had shared.

"You are my wife," he said. "I will be the one to hold the door for you. No other man need serve you."

"Very possessive for a man who isn't sure what he wants."

They said nothing more, because then they reached the top of the steps, and were ushered inside, where they were announced grandly, and in a fashion that Mauro would have taken a great kind of satisfaction in under any other circumstances.

He was here. Standing at the top, all these people he had looked up to all of his life, people who had kept him shut out of society, gaz-ing up at him, as if he were the most important and powerful man in the room. Unlikely though he was, even without the inclusion of his new, royal bride.

But she brought that blue-blooded element he could not manufacture on his own.

She was carrying his child, a child who was the future ruler of a nation.

Nothing could elevate him more.

And yet, that wasn't the primary focus of his thoughts.

Mostly, he was thinking about her. Mostly, he was remembering the way her skin had felt beneath his hands.

The way she had sighed and moaned when he had kissed her. A pang of resentment hit him in the chest. That she should have such power over him. Over this moment.

He tightened his hold on her, her ultimatum ringing in his head.

They made their way down the stairs, into the center of the tangled knot of crows masquerading as aristocracy. Black dresses on the reed-thin bodies of the women, black tuxes and ties on the men.

Except for Astrid. Who was like liquid gold, shimmering before them all.

A prize. That was what he had fashioned her into. And yet, no matter how much he repeated that to himself as they circulated the room, as they made readings to those around them, Astrid with her royal ease, and him entirely absent of such a thing, all he could think was that he had revealed himself in many ways by his choices tonight.

Revealed the fact that he was not of the aristocracy, no matter that he shared half of his blood with it.

Because no one else would have dressed their wife as such an obvious prize, only to flaunt her importance.

And yet, she was beautiful. And she deserved to look as she did. As the most expensive, glorious woman in the room, and why should he have dressed her as anything else? Subtlety, he decided, might be best left to those born with money. He was not going to concern himself with it.

That was when he saw *him*.

Impossible to miss him. Broad shouldered, and taller than most of the men in the room, except for Mauro himself.

Age had not stooped the man's shoulders, and Mauro supposed that if he weren't quite so enraged at the mere existence of him, he might appreciate what that said about his genetics.

Instead, he only felt his stomach turned sour with the injustice of it all. Because his mother was dead and gone, and this man was able to stand tall, proud, well dressed and with his wife, as if he had not caused immeasurable pain over the course of years.

As if nothing troubled his conscience at all.

His eyes caught Mauro's and held them, and he whispered something to the woman at his side, who nodded in dutiful obedience, and separated from her husband, moving off to a cluster of women standing next to a tray of champagne.

Mauro gritted his teeth. "Well, it has been some time."

"Has it? I wasn't sure if we had ever met," his father returned.

"We did. I was a child. You had me thrown straight back to the slum I came out of."

"Oh, was that you? It's difficult for me to keep my slum bastards straight."

"And yet, you seem to know me well enough now."

"You've done well for yourself," he said, casting an eye over Astrid.

Mauro bitterly regretted involving her in this, the moment the old man's eyes began to roam over her luxurious curves.

Astrid, on the other hand, didn't seem regretful in the least. Astrid faced his father head-on.

"I'm Queen Astrid von Bjornland," she said, her tone frosty, her shoulders straight. Her hold on him tight. "I do not believe we've met."

"Dominic Farenzi, Duke of San Isabella."

"I see. And you are connected to my husband through accident of birth?"

She sounded perfectly civil, but he could sense she was feeling anything but.

"Yes. I had the impression you were connected to my bastard son much the same way."

Her lips curved upward. "Oh, no. I chose him. I chose him quite deliberately to be the father of my child. My heir. Because he is perfect, and everything I could possibly want, from a genetic standpoint and otherwise."

"I didn't realize the standards of perfection were lowered so."

"If this is the way that you expected you might leverage me and my status for your own personal benefit when you sought to announce your connection to my husband, you have badly miscalculated."

"You assumed it was about you? How very fascinating."

"I am queen of an entire nation. I assume many things are about me, and I've yet to be proven wrong."

"Is this what you have become?" his father asked. "Because at least when you were a boy you spoke for yourself. Now, you have this woman speaking for you." He shook his head. "But then, I am not surprised. It is the only thing that gave you any relevance in the eyes of the media, and truly in the eyes of the world. One sin peddler is essentially the same as any other. You are not only uninteresting on your own, but unoriginal."

Mauro chuckled, and before he could grab hold of his composure, reached out and grabbed hold of his father's throat. "I see. I'm very sorry that I failed to produce a surprise for you." He chuckled. "But you should understand this. If you assume that you understand me, you will be bitterly disappointed. And if you think you can stand here and speak to my wife, speak about my wife, and face no repercussion, then you truly know nothing about me at all. I have done a great many things in my life that were rooted in calculation and self-service. But Astrid is mine. Mine. And unlike you, I keep what is mine. My child. My woman. You will not speak to her. You will not speak about her. You will not sell any more of your torrid stories to the press about my mother. If you do anything to cause Astrid harm, I will end you. Financially. Physically if I must. You could only lord things over me when I was a little boy who had need. You could only cow me, control me as long as you had more power than I did. The tide has shifted, Father. And now that I've made my position clear, all that's left to do is for you to decide whether or not you want to push me. I would suggest that you don't."

He released his hold on the old man, rage

coursing through his body. And he felt Astrid's calming touch on his shoulder. He looked at her, the red, foggy haze of his vision beginning to clear, and he saw that her expression was filled with concern. "Mauro..."

"You reveal yourself," his father said. "That you would stoop to physical threats. You might be able to put on a suit, earn money, spend money, but you will always be what you were born. The son of a whore."

"Push me any harder and I may be the son of a dead man."

"Oh, I have no doubt. I have no interest in pushing you. I'm just making it clear, whatever narrative you think is happening, it is blood that wins. Time and time again."

"You're right about that," Mauro said. "It is blood that wins out in the end. And when mine triumphs, you had best hope it's not due to the fact that I spilled any of yours." He looked over at Astrid, who had gone pale. "Come, *cara*. I think that our time at this event has lapsed."

He had no more time for this. Had no more desire to engage in such a farce. He was going to end the evening now, and he was going to end it exactly the way he had intended on ending it before this miserable farce had began. She would see who he was.

He pulled her through the crowd, not caring that they had drawn curious stares. That they were now being subjected to scrutiny by all around them. He didn't care. He was not a good man. He was not a civilized man. He was not one of them. If it had not been apparent before, then it was apparent now.

He was Mauro Bianchi, and he was from the slums. If blood won out, then he was quite all right letting it show freely.

He signaled his driver using his phone, and by the time they reached the front of the hotel, the limo was there waiting for them. He ushered her inside, and she said nothing. That was unusual, as Astrid typically had a comment, or a snarky aside. Right now she seemed to have nothing.

Perhaps he truly had made her realize who he was. Made her realize what he was.

Now, perhaps she would find it undeniable. "I've made my decision," he said, once the limo began to move away from the hotel. "You're mine. There will be no discussion about any alternatives."

CHAPTER ELEVEN

ASTRID WAS STILL shell-shocked by the time they tumbled out of the limo and into the lobby of the apartment building that housed Mauro's penthouse. The way that his father had treated him, the way that he had treated his father...

She didn't know why she had expected anything else, actually. Mauro had all the trappings of a civilized man, but she had always known that underneath that exterior beat the heart of a barbarian.

She had not been disappointed in tonight's showing. Not on that score.

And then the way that he had... Declared his possession of her when they had gotten back into the car. But then, he hadn't spoken again. And he had not touched her.

She fidgeted, feeling restless as they stood in the lobby for a moment. Mauro seemed to take stock of his surroundings, looking for paparazzi, she wondered, and then he dragged her to the lift, the doors opening wide, as he moved them both inside. And that was when she discovered what he truly meant by being his.

He pushed her against the wall, the metal biting into her shoulder blades as he did. Then he gripped her chin between his thumb and forefinger and held her steady. His eyes blazing down into hers. He was like a wild animal. A feral beast that she could neither soothe nor tame. One that looked completely and utterly bent on having her at his mercy.

She resisted. Everything in her resisted, because hadn't she been resisting such a thing for her entire life?

Until him. He was the beginning of that. The awakening of that desire. Feel a man's strength. To allow it to carry her own, if only for a little while. And now, even more, the temptation to allow it to overwhelm her utterly and completely.

It was intoxicating. To think that perhaps she truly could be his. She had belonged to causes.

To an entire country worth of people. She belonged to Bjornland, she belonged to her duty. But to find another person who could carry all of that was a distantly hazy fantasy that she hadn't even been aware she'd ever possessed. She wanted it.

But she wasn't sure she was brave enough.

But she could see in him the anger, force, the will to bend her. To create the space that would require that submission. A space that would hold her. A space that would sustain her.

So when he kissed her mouth, she kissed him back, with all the ferocity penned up inside of her. There was no small amount of it. It was real and raw and wild. Something she had imagined might be beyond her.

But she didn't feel like another entity, not like another creature, no. Instead, she felt like she might be the truest, rawest form of Astrid. With no parents watching her every move, no press. No brother. No assistant. No council of angry men opposing her very existence.

As if she lived in a world created just for her, just for Mauro.

Not in the way she had felt when she had

been pretending to be someone else, no. She felt like her. Like she was truly at home in her skin for the first time. Like she had become real, and now nothing on earth would ever be able to make her unreal. The elevator stopped, and the doors slid open, revealing his sleek and lovely penthouse, as light and view conscious as his office, with windows that she had been assured were made with one-way glass.

Affording him the view that he wanted, giving him the privacy he needed. As if reading her mind, he led her over to the window, and positioned her in front of him.

"Look at all that," he said. "All those glittering lights below. I can buy every single place and person those lights represent. Everyone. Here I am on top. And I have you."

She shivered, and he moved her hair to the side, exposing the nape of her neck. Leaning forward and pressing a firm kiss to her skin. "Yes. I have you. I want you to take that dress off."

Heat crept into her face. "Here? In front of the windows?"

"I already told you… No one can see," he

said, his hand traveling down the line of her spine, stroking gently. He grasped the zipper tab that rested low on her back. "I want to see."

He drew it down slowly, the fabric parting, going loose and dropping from her shoulders, down to her hips, before it slid the rest of the way down to the floor.

The underwear she had on was whisper thin, barely there, and exposed the entirety of her backside for his enjoyment. Something he made no secret of as he reached out and grabbed her, squeezed her, growling in his appreciation.

"You're very beautiful," he said. "A beautiful trophy. All for me."

His words, rough and angry, should have upset her. Should have made her feel small and used. Instead, they sent a thrill through her body.

She was a great many things, but she had never been someone's trophy. She supposed it should make her unhappy.

But she was a woman with a great deal of power.

And within the broad scope of that power, knowing that she could call bodyguards in here at any moment and have Mauro dispatched handily. That she had an entire military at her command… That she had faced down leaders, heads of state and a great many men who had not wanted her in the position she held.

Yes, given all that, she could think of very little that made her feel threatened. It allowed her to sink into this. Allowed her to embrace it.

To give herself a moment where she was nothing more than an object for his enjoyment. A gift for him.

"I like this," he said softly, stroking her in the center of her back again. "My city laid out before me. My woman, laid out before me."

He advanced on her, pushing her closer to the glass, until her hip bones connected with the cool, smooth surface, her stomach, her breasts. Her thighs. Her palms were rested flat against it, and she looked out, having the strangest sensation that she was flying.

"You even carry my baby inside you," he

said, his voice getting impossibly rough now. "You are mine. Mine. In every beautiful, twisted-up way you possibly could be." He kissed her neck, her shoulder, gripping her hip, then the other as he continued to kiss her, tracing a line down to the waistband of her panties. He hooked his fingers in the waistband, tugging them down, before rising back to his feet and unhooking her bra, leaving her now completely naked, pressed against the glass. "The world is at your feet, my Queen," he whispered. "And I want you at mine."

He whirled her around so that she was facing him, the glass cold on her back. There was something about it that felt dangerous. This razor-thin pane between herself and the air outside. Between falling endlessly and safety. She began to work his clothes next. Wordlessly. In absolute obedience to his command. She undid his tie. Pushed his jacket from his shoulders and let it fall to the floor. She undid his shirt, her knees bending slightly with each button she pushed through the hole.

And then she did end up on her knees before him.

Ready to give him what she had last night. And more. Everything he wanted. All of her. She undid his belt, his pants slowly, taking his length in her hand and testing him, curling her fingers around all that heavy weight. He wrapped his own hand around himself, and pressed against her lips. She complied, opening to him. Taking him inside.

He bucked his hips forward slightly, gently, and she relaxed, allowing him to set the pace. Trusting him. Giving herself over to him.

He was big and strong, and he could hurt her if he chose to. But she didn't put up any defenses. She didn't do anything to protect herself.

She had seen what he was earlier, and still, she knelt before him, offering him her throat, though she had seen him grab a man by his earlier.

His movements became less measured, more intense, and she let her head fall back against the glass as he found his pleasure, accepted his release as a strange, warm sense of satisfaction rolled through her.

She had been of service to him.

The idea made her giggle. And she didn't giggle. Particularly not after things like that.

She was buzzing, fuzzy. She looked at his body and saw that for now he was satisfied, but she found herself being pulled to her feet, lifted up into his arms. He clamped one arm around her waist, and urged her legs up around his hips, as he walked her back toward the bedroom. It wasn't any less private than the other room, large windows dominating the walls in there, as well. But there was the bed. Large and spare, with a low black headboard and a stark black bedspread.

"You will look beautiful against my sheets," he said, his voice low and harsh. "I wish to look at you." She moved over to the edge of the bed, uncertain as to how to proceed. "On your knees, facing the headboard."

She hurried to obey, getting into the center of the mattress and arching her back slightly, allowing him the full view of her body. He reached forward, pressing his fingers between her legs and teasing her where she knew she was slick with need for him.

"Turn around," he ordered.

She obeyed, still on all fours, but facing him now. She could see that he was hard again, ready for her already.

"Lie down on your back," he said. "And part your thighs for me."

Again, she did as he bid, lying back against the velvet bed cover and opening herself to him. Keeping nothing back.

She was trembling, her entire body shaking with the force of the strangeness of all of this. Of what it meant to give this kind of control.

"There," he said. "I like that. Just as I suspected. This was meant to be. You were meant to be mine."

"I am yours," she said. It felt like the right thing to say. And judging by the glint in his eye, it had been.

"You know," he said. "I told myself after that first time I met my father that I would never, ever allow myself to want without having. Ever again." He reached out, pressing his hand against her stomach, smoothing it gently over the slightly rounded bump there. "And so, I will spend my life having you, then. Because the alternative is to want endlessly, and I refuse it. I will not."

"Let me satisfy you," she said.

He growled, joining her on the bed, positioning himself between her legs and sliding inside her easily.

She gasped, arching upward, joining him in an intense, shaky rhythm that she thought might just break her apart. Might destroy them both. But she couldn't see another alternative. She needed him. Needed this.

She wrapped her legs around him and let him give all his weight to her.

And that was when she realized. The way that it worked. The push and the pull. The way he held her, kept her safe, and the way that she became the resting place for him.

Domination. Submission. Give. Take.

"Mine," he growled, as he stiffened above her, his body pulsing inside her. "Mine."

That last, possessive declaration drove her over the edge, her release going off like a shower of sparks inside her.

And when it was through, she was shaking. Spent.

Weaker.

Stronger.

When it was through, she was his.

There would be no force on earth that could ever undo it.

"I hope you don't mind," Astrid said the next morning, sitting in the center of his bed with the regal bearing of an empress. The blankets were bunched up around her, her breasts exposed, her red hair tumbled down over her shoulders. She was clutching a coffee mug and managed to make it all look effortless and elegant.

She was such a compelling acquisition.

There was nothing, and no one, that had ever been part of his life who was quite so lovely or rare.

"You hope I don't mind what?" He was standing across the room from her, still completely naked, and he took satisfaction from the clear fact that she was enjoying the sight of him.

"I had a doctor's appointment settled in Bjornland. And, as we are here, I figured it would be easier to just have the doctor bring her equipment to us."

"Did you?"

"I didn't know when you would be through with your business here. I could have flown back, but Dr. Yang is going to meet us here instead. She's the best obstetrician in Europe, and we were going to have to fly her to be on loan anyway. Instead, she'll be bringing her equipment to us."

"My penthouse is going to be transformed into a clinic?"

"Yes," she said. "There is nothing untoward about it. People give birth at home. I might as well have my examinations done in a similarly comfortable environment. And, we won't have to contend with paparazzi."

"When do you expect her arrival? As I'm not the one meant to be in the hospital gown, perhaps I should get dressed." He bent down and retrieved his pair of dark slacks from the floor, where they had left them last night.

"Yes, perhaps you might want to do that."

"Though, we may have some time…"

It was only an hour later when the doctor

showed up, and thankfully, Mauro had been able to put his legendary focus to the task and leave Astrid doubly satisfied by the time the doctor arrived. She had a warm bedside manner, and an efficiency to her movements that would have come across as brusque with most people, but with Dr. Yang it came across as a kindness. As if the time of the patient was being considered and respected.

He could see why Astrid had gone to the trouble of bringing her all this way.

"How have you been feeling?" the doctor asked.

"Well," Astrid said. "Surprisingly well. Only a bit of fatigue, and occasional nausea in the mornings, but nothing extreme."

If Astrid had been feeling nauseous this morning, she had hidden it well, and said nothing. The same with her fatigue. She was such a strong, self-contained woman, and he suddenly found himself overcome by the desire to bear some of that burden. To make it so she did not hide such things from him.

It was an ache that hit him square in the

chest. A walnut-sized pain that rested there like a knot.

He didn't like it. Not one bit.

"Date of your last period?" the doctor asked.

Astrid rattled off the date effortlessly.

"Date of last intercourse?"

Astrid's face turned dark red. "That would be today's date."

The doctor didn't react to this, but Astrid was the color of a royal tomato, and Mauro took some amusement in that. It was a sweet thing, the way something like that could make her blush. It spoke of her inexperience, and of the fact that what was between them was somewhat singular.

Maybe even a bit miraculous.

That word, *miraculous*, was reinforced when the doctor had Astrid lie back on the bed and expose her stomach, squeezing some warmed gel onto it, where it was slightly distended. Then she placed the wand onto her skin and moved around, watery noise filling the room. The watery sound turned into a wish and whisper, steady and fast.

"And that's the heartbeat," she said. "Very

238 THE QUEEN'S BABY SCANDAL

strong. Sounds good." She moved the wand around. "It is a little bit early, but since you are sixteen weeks, we might be able to see the baby's gender. If you're interested."

"I am," Astrid said, her expression taking on a dreamy quality.

"I don't mind either way," he said. "As long as the child is healthy. It doesn't matter to me what gender." Dr. Yang and Astrid exchanged a glance, but he could not decode what it meant.

"Let me see," she said.

Suddenly, everything came into focus. The baby's head. An arm. A foot, which kicked as the doctor brought the wand down around the baby's body.

"It doesn't wish to be disturbed," Mauro said, that pit in his chest expanding, growing. As if a tree was growing from that walnut now. Becoming something large and hard and completely unmanageable.

"The baby doesn't mind," Dr. Yang said. "It's good that the baby is responsive. That's what we like to see."

He didn't know if he wanted to see it at all.

It was suddenly so very real. This human inside Astrid. A child.

His child.

"We are in luck," she said. "There we go. We have a perfect view. You're having a son."

The mix of emotion on Astrid's face was strange. "I'm glad in some ways," she said. "His road will be easier. It's easier to be king."

"I would have liked to rub their faces in the fact that I was having a girl though."

She laughed. "That's a terrible reason to wish for one or the other."

He could understand what she was saying, and even the significance in her world. Producing a male heir was traditionally a valued thing. And Astrid herself was a defiance of that. But he couldn't think of that. Not now. All he could think of was that he was having a son.

A son.

A little boy, like the one his own father had taunted and sent away. A boy who would possibly look like him. Possibly look like his old man.

Redemption.

In a thousand strange and wonderful ways, this was redemption. He craved it. And with that craving came something deep and unpleasant. Something he told himself he would not feel. Not again. This deep unending need for something he couldn't even define. This child made him hurt. And the woman in front of him, with her eyes shining so bright, she made him ache.

He felt as if his whole life had been turned inside out.

And he had been driven, driven to claim her, driven to claim the baby. He had been motivated by something he couldn't even put words to, but here in this small space, with that little life flickering on the screen in front of him, with that deep truth attached to him.

A boy.

A son.

That drive met with something different. Something dangerous. Something that had the power to wound and destroy. Something that he had told himself he wanted no part of for all that time.

It made no sense. He had her. Right here. He had the baby right here. So why did it hurt like this? Why? He could not fathom it.

"Congratulations," Dr. Yang said. She put her hand on Mauro's shoulder, and somehow in her expression he saw a wealth of things. Perhaps even sympathy, and he couldn't understand why she would feel sorry for him. Except that perhaps his own confusion was visible on his face. He despised that too. He was not a man given to confusion. He was not a man given to indecisiveness. Astrid had done something to him. She had… Damaged him in some way. And he hated it. He hated it.

"All right. I'll give you a moment with each other, and to get dressed, and then I will have everything cleared from here, and leave you alone. The child is healthy. Congratulations."

And with that, she left them. Astrid sat up, wiping the jelly from her stomach with a warm cloth that had been placed by the bedside. "I expected that we would get to find out it was a boy. Not so soon. I'm glad… I'm glad we were together when we found out."

"You are happy?" he asked. The idea of her being unhappy with his son upset him even more than the idea of his own conflicted feelings.

"Yes," she said. "Really, his life will be easier. Easier because he's a boy. Easier because he won't have opposition to him. And I suppose what I hoped for was a chance to test out just how much we could modernize the country. But I cannot stand in his way for his gender any more than my father should have doubted me for mine. He will be a good king. We'll raise him to be."

They would raise him. Yes. They would. Of course they would. He gritted his teeth, squaring his jaw. "Yes."

"Are you all right?"

"I'm fine."

"I'm glad we're doing this together," she said. "I think I really wouldn't have wanted to do it alone.

"You won't be alone," he said, trying to harden his heart against the words.

"I guess not. Technically. I would've had nannies, and whatever else. But I am glad. I'm glad to have you. I'm glad our child will have you. Because a nanny is no substitute for a father. And what I did I did without thinking about the people involved. Not just you. But our child. It wasn't only you I would have deprived. And I'm glad things are like this. I'm glad that we'll be… I'm glad we'll be a family."

That word made him feel like he'd been cracked open. And after she spoke them, Mauro couldn't think of a single thing to say.

CHAPTER TWELVE

MAURO HAD GONE off to work quickly after the doctor visit, and Astrid knew that something wasn't quite right, but she also could not for the life of her figure out what to do about it.

Perhaps, Mauro had legitimately needed to go into the office. That was entirely possible. Or perhaps he was running from something, which she also suspected might be true, but didn't have a clue as to what she was supposed to do if that was the case.

The idea of him running was a strange one, but in many ways she understood. She had never been more terrified in her entire life than she was when she had seen that baby. So real and vivid on the ultrasound screen. A boy. Their son. There was something undeniable about that. Something real and heavy. And if he needed a moment alone after, she would have certainly understood.

Of course, he would likely rather die than admit that.

Which is why, she suspected, he had simply excused himself.

Because the man was too alpha to function, and God forbid he have a feeling in her presence.

That very thought made a smile that curved her lips upward. She supposed the same could be said about her.

But he made her want to be not quite so soft. Not quite so stubborn and closed off.

She wondered if he needed something from her now, and simply didn't have the ability to express it.

Then she wondered why on earth she was thinking about him when she had just gotten such momentous news about her life, her future. She was having a boy. That should consume her thoughts. Utterly and totally. And yet, she found that she was consumed with him.

She was lately. Quite a bit.

She had… Feelings for him.

If she was honest with herself she had for an impossible amount of time.

She had felt a strange sort of connection with him just looking at his pictures, and while she had initially told herself it was a response to his genetics, and then had told herself it was chemistry, now she wondered if it was something more. Something that made no sense at all.

And if it hadn't been since looking at the photos, it was definitely since the first time they had made love.

The way that he touched her. The way that he made her feel… It was all a strange kind of magic. He made her feel happy to be a woman, made her glory in the way that she had been made. Made her feel as if she understood and embraced her femininity for the first time, really and truly. When Mauro finally did arrive home, he was distant. He shut himself in his home office for a time, coming out only to ask if she was hungry for dinner.

When she said that she was, he set about cooking in the small, high-gloss kitchen. She watched his movements, sure and confident as he set about preparing their food.

"I didn't know you cooked," she said.

"I'm quite accomplished at it," he said. "I can make a fairly gourmet meal out of deeply underwhelming ingredients. A skill I picked up as a boy. Of course, now I prefer to make truly wonderful food out of excellent ingredients. It's always nice when you have the option."

"Well," she said. "Yes."

"I hope you like filet mignon."

"I think I can make do," she said, smiling. "I don't know how to cook. I've never had to do it. Everyone always does it for me. And I've never seen the point in picking up a skill when it can just as easily be done."

"Sometimes it's simply good to have the skill for the sake of it," he pointed out.

"I suppose. But there's always been… An idea around me that I could concern myself with more important things. And anything that's trivial… Well, anything that's a triviality I can leave to other people."

"I can see how feeding yourself might be considered trivial," he said drily.

"Well, you don't have to be ridiculous about it."

"I'm not being ridiculous. I'm being practical."

"What are you making? In all your practicality?"

"Filet mignon with a red wine reduction. And mixed steamed vegetables. Truly. Nothing overly elaborate."

"It all seems elaborate to me," she said.

She sat back and watched him work, not at all goaded into getting up and helping simply because he had taunted her about not knowing how to cook. She enjoyed watching him work. Anyway, she was a bit fatigued. Not terribly, but just a bit more than she was used to. But this time away with him had been... Well, it had been nice. Like a snippet of another life. A life she could have had if she had been just a regular woman. One who had met a man and fallen in love by chance.

In love? Was that what this was?

Her mind went blank for a moment, nothing

there except for that one word, heavy, terrifying, looming above her.

Love.

Did she *love* him?

Her first instinct was to push it down. To hide. To never, ever admit to herself that she felt these things, let alone admit it to him.

But she saw clearly, suddenly, the fabric of her life. Her parents. Her mother's ferocity, and her unfailing need for Astrid to succeed, and her father's cool indifference.

And both of those things had a wall. A firm wall between her and Astrid. She was ideological for her mother. A point of contention for her father. And they had loved her. They had.

She supposed.

But the layers that kept them back from her... Pride. All of it was protective. And it had taught her to do the same. It was what she'd always done, and so much of it was because of her position, easy to sink into naturally. But so much of it had been to protect herself. From scrutiny, from criticism. From disappointing her mother, from failing in the eyes of her father, when he so clearly imagined that she would.

It all became so clear right then.

That no wall had ever healed. That no wall had ever truly protected. She had been concerned, from the beginning, that Mauro was the barbarian at the gate. But she had not imagined how apt that description was. Not really. And something had to change. Something inside her. It had begun, all those months ago, with that trip to the club.

Continued as they had grown intimate, as they had given and taken from each other, as she had found power in her surrender.

And perhaps now this was the next stage of that lesson. Strength in vulnerability.

In becoming the one thing she had always feared she might be.

Weak. Vulnerable. Open.

But perhaps it was the only way. Perhaps, it was the only path to what was real.

Something she had not considered, not truly, as she had started out this journey, was the fact that it was about more than simply gaining independence from a council. It was about more than living in defiance of her father's last-ditch effort to control her. It was about becoming more of a person than a figurehead. It was about defying some of what her mother had instilled in her, as well. The need to be perfect. The need to be a symbol.

She didn't want to be a symbol to her son. She wanted to be his mother. She didn't want to live her life as someone worthy of being carved onto a coin. She wanted to live her life. To do the best she could. To be the best she could, but to be her. To be Astrid von Bjorn-land, as she was. As she was meant to be.

Not in a constant state of trying to prove herself, not in an eternal struggle to appear worthy. No. She wanted to be herself.

She was flawed. She was strong. She was weak. She was angry. She was in love. She was filled with hope for the future, and terror about it, as well.

She was everything, not simply one thing.

And it would start here. It had to start here.

"Mauro," she said slowly. "I love you."

He barely paused in his movements. "That's only because I'm cooking steak for you."

She shook her head. "No. I am in love with you. I have been. For quite some time. And today… The ultrasound, the baby… All of it crystallized something for me. I cannot be the mother that I want to be, the ruler I want to be, the woman I want to be. If I'm going to be the best mother, the best ruler, the best wife, then I have to… I have to be different. I have to break the cycle."

"What cycle?"

"This cycle where I care only for my own feelings. Honestly, that I gave even a moment's thought to wishing he was a girl, to further my own cause, this cause that I've been fighting all of my life. It shows me that my parents impacted me in ways I wish they hadn't. I know my mother did. She meant well. She believed in me. But I was a battleground. I don't want to do that to our child. I don't want to live that way with you. I don't want to live the way my parents did. I want something more. I'm willing to give whatever I need to, to make that happen. I love you, and I think that… We can be happy. I think we can be wonderful, not just an arrangement. I think we could be everything."

He turned away from her, and went back to cooking, saying nothing. Doing nothing.

"The food is finished," he said, putting the steak on a plate and dishing vegetables beside it. "Let's eat."

There with him in the dining room in stunned silence, trying to focus, while emotions were spinning through her like cracks of light. Finally, she stood.

"I'm afraid," she said. "I have been. That my father was secretly right. I wasn't strong. That's why I never doubted myself. I couldn't afford to. Why I went forward with my crazy plan to trick you into getting me pregnant. Because I had gotten myself to a place where I was so convinced that anything that I might want was a betrayal of what I needed to be. Well, I'm not doing it. Not anymore. I'm afraid. I'm afraid I won't do a good job. But I'm doing it anyway. I'm afraid I won't be a good mother. I'm afraid you will leave me. But I… I want it enough for me. For us."

He said nothing, only assessed her with cool,

dark eyes. She moved down the table to where he sat. And, heart hammering in her chest, desperation pouring into her like a fountain, she dropped to her knees in front of him. "I'm your servant," she said. "Let me give you what you need."

CHAPTER THIRTEEN

MAURO COULDN'T BREATHE. He couldn't think. He had spent the entire day away at the office for a reason.

Because everything with Astrid, with the baby, had simply been too much for him to take on board. It had been too much for him to handle. And now this. Now she was throwing herself at his feet, confessing love, prostrate before him. And worst of all, worse than watching her kneel before him, was the fact that it intensified the growing ache inside.

He couldn't even blame the child, which ultimately he had rationalized as being a natural response. Very few men faced impending fatherhood without some sort of panic. But that wasn't it.

It was her. She did this to him.

And then, she began to strip off the dress

she was wearing, began to reveal her body, and he could not turn away.

"Whatever you need from me... Let me give it. Let *me* be everything you need."

It was so perilously close to what he had wished he could get from her earlier today. That he could see that vulnerability, that he could understand what scared her, what drove her, what made her. And now, it was as if she was showing him, but not only that, was asking him to do the same.

He wanted her to stop. Wanted to tell her enough was enough.

Yet he found it impossible to turn away, especially as she revealed those pale, perfect breasts for inspection, especially when all of her soft, silky beauty was laid out before him. She took everything off except for her shoes, just as she had done that first night they were together.

She stretched out on her back, on the floor in front of him, her arms lifted over her head, her wrists crossed, her knees locked criminally together, as if it might spare some of her modesty. And he no longer hungered for the food on his plate. No. All the hunger he possessed was for her. Utterly. His desire like a living thing roaring through his body, right now.

No.

Part of him wanted to run away from, from that feeling she created inside, but that same part of himself would not allow it. Would not allow for him to admit she did strange and dark, magical things that no one else had ever done.

She terrified him. Him. A man who had sold his body to survive, who had spent nights sleeping on the street, wondering if the wrong kind of people would find him, and if he would wake up at all.

He feared nothing. And yet this one, fragile queen seemed to have the power to tear him apart from the inside out.

This woman who seemed to be able to give and take in equal measure. Who seemed to be able to take charge and then give her power over at will.

He didn't understand.

He did not understand how she had spoken to him as she had, so raw and real and broken. So revealing. As if she were bulletproof. When he could see full well she was not. All that tender skin so very capable of being destroyed.

And yet… Yet. He dropped to his knees, forced her thighs apart, exposed all of that luscious body of hers.

He should turn away. Should not take her in his current state of mind. It took all of his strength to even admit that. That she'd pushed him to this place.

And he had none left to resist.

He touched her breasts, her stomach, that tender place between her legs. Let himself drink in every inch of her beauty.

He held himself back, keeping a distance between them as he undid the closure on his slacks.

He gripped himself, stroking his hardened length twice while looking down at her.

Then he reached down, gripping her thigh and draping her leg up over his shoulder, repeating the motion with the other.

Then he rocked forward, one arm like a bar over her thighs as he gripped himself with his free hand and slid himself over the slick entrance of her body, before pressing his arousal against her opening.

She gasped, letting her head fall back, and he lost himself. Poured every emotion, every pain, every deep sharp jagged thing that was making him feel, into her. He wrapped them up, let it cut them both, and he let them both get lost in the animal need that was driving him forward, making him into a thing he didn't recognize. A thing he feared was closer to real than anything he'd allowed himself to feel for decades.

And when he came, it was on a ferocious roar, with a bastard's body pulsing around his.

And he thought that maybe, just maybe, that had fixed things. That it had drowned everything else out. But then, she lifted her hand and touched his face.

"I love you."

And he could not endure it.

Astrid could tell the moment that she had lost him. The moment when she had pushed too far.

But what could they do? What could she do?

She loved him. They were married. She was having his baby. They were bonded, whether he wanted that to be true or not. And she could see something more than a lack of love in his eyes. That wasn't what she saw there at all. It was anguish. It was fear. It was abject terror. And desire. A deep, unending desire.

To take what she had offered, she was certain of it. And yet, something was holding him back. She couldn't figure out what it was, couldn't quite say where the fear was coming from, only that it was there.

"Don't do this," she said softly.

"Don't," he said. "Don't act like you can read my mind because you shared my bed. Any number of women have done this with me."

She stayed right where she was on the floor. "Any number of women have submitted themselves to you completely?"

"It is only sex," he said.

"Is it? Because it seems to be something that terrifies you. I love you," she said it again.

"That isn't what I want," he said.

"I don't care what you want."

"No. You never have, have you? You find

it so easy to make proclamations, to say that you're going to change because you now realize the error of your selfish, entitled ways, but you don't actually intend to do it, do you? Because the moment that it becomes inconvenient for you, you begin to tell other people they are wrong."

"That isn't what I've done," she said, pushing back, indignation and anger filling her. "I love you, Mauro, and if that offends you so very much you might want to ask yourself why."

"That is not what I signed on for when I signed on for this marriage."

"Yes. You only signed on for forever and said that I was yours. Why would I think a little thing like love would be a simple thing for you to accept?"

"You say that you want nothing, but in the end, you will," he said. "Nothing that I do will be enough for you, now that you've entered love into the equation."

"That sounds like baggage that we haven't discussed," she said flatly. "Because I never asked for a damn thing."

"This is not the way that I operate. It is not what I do."

"No," she said. "I know. You've done anything and everything to build yourself this tower. This place where you can look down on the world. And you seem to be fine as long as we can play games, and you can look down on me when I'm naked, and I give you everything that you desire. But now that I'm telling you there's more, now that I'm telling you I want more, you find that to be a problem?"

"You're asking for the impossible. You're asking for something I can't give," he said, his voice hard. "I don't love."

"You're not going to love our child?"

"Dammit. I already do," he said, his voice hoarse. "But I…"

"But you can't love too many people, is that it? You can't open your heart any farther? Because you might be hurt?"

"You don't understand. I had to make myself hard. I had to build myself a tower, because no one would take care of me. My mother loved me, and she did the best she could, but when she was whoring herself out, she didn't exactly enact a screening process to make sure that none of the men she brought into her home tried something with her son. And no, none of them ever succeeded, but it wasn't for lack of trying. Yes, I had to become hard. So you cannot ask for me to open up my heart on command. I'm not even certain it's possible. More than that, I'm not certain I want to. I want to have this arrangement."

"More fortification. That's what you want. You marry me, you get that."

"That is not why I married you."

"You married me for our child," she said. "And certainly not anything to do with the fact that you keep hoping if you put enough Band-Aids on this wound you'll be all right."

"I am an infamous playboy," he said, his tone hard. "I am legendary for my ability to sleep with women and move on. What makes you think you're any different?"

"I know I'm different," she said. "I am a queen, and not just that, but I am *your* queen. You are the only man that I have ever knelt before, and the only man that I ever will kneel before. But until you can set down your own pride, and you can make yourself honest, afraid, vulnerable, we can't ever be. You're right about that."

"Are you issuing ultimatums?"

"Yes. As I said before, we had to either be forever or not at all. But to me, now forever is about love. Because I lived in a family where pride and stubbornness won. I lived in a home where there wasn't…love. Not really. I won't treat our child to the same. I will not. I won't treat you to the same. I deserved more. I deserve more, and I didn't get it. Because those around me were content to let it be. While I am not. Not anymore."

"And what will you do if I say no?"

"I will get on my private jet and I will fly back to Bjornland. You may come and see me again when the baby is born. But you and I are not a couple."

"I will not allow you to keep the marriage. I will not allow you to keep your front for the benefit of the world."

"I don't care. Or have you not been listening? I don't care anymore. It isn't about image. None of this is about image. I want you. I love you. I don't care how it looks. I don't give a damn if you were a prostitute. I don't care who your mother was. I don't care who your father is. I care about us. I care about our baby. I care about what we could be. And how much happiness we could have. How much more we could have."

She touched his face. "You were fearless once. You climbed up to your father's house and faced him when you were a boy, not having any idea what you might get in return. I'm standing here guaranteeing that you will have me. All you have to do is say yes."

"No," he said. "The divorce papers will be in the mail."

"Mauro…"

Astrid had to make good on her promise. And in her last act of paying heed to appearances, she squared her shoulders, and held her head high. She collected her clothing, and dressed in front of him, hiding nothing. Then she walked out of his apartment, out of his life.

And only when she was in her plane, up in the air and alone, did she let herself weep.

But she knew she had made the right choice.

Because she was the queen of so many. The hope of a nation.

But to Mauro, she had been a woman. To Mauro, she had been Astrid.

And Astrid wanted his *love*.

She would settle for nothing less.

Mauro was a study in misery, and he stubbornly refused to believe that he had any recourse in the matter. Astrid was being unreasonable. He called his lawyer in the middle of the night, in a fit of rage, and had divorce papers drafted.

And then had spent the next three days doing nothing with them. Nothing at all. The view from his office window was tainted, and he hated it all now because of her. Because of what she'd said. That he was using it to look down and hold himself above.

"Mr. Bianchi…"

He turned around to see Carlo rushing nervously into the room, with Gunnar von Bjornland striding in front of him.

"What are you doing here?" he asked his soon-to-be former brother-in-law.

"I should think that was quite obvious. Oh, but then I forget you don't know that I have a gun hidden in my jacket."

"Are you threatening me?"

"Yes. I knew that you would hurt my sister."

"To the contrary, your sister walked away from me."

"Astrid is a sensible woman. If she walked away from you, she had a reason."

"Yes, your sister is just so damn sensible. So sensible that she sneaked away from her minders, went to one of my clubs and tricked me into getting her pregnant. Then married me. Then left me when I refused to produce the correct words of love on command. Truly, it is a miracle that I was able to walk away from such a creature."

"I will concede that her tricking you into getting her pregnant is a problem. The rest… Why don't you love her? Everyone should."

The words hit him square in the chest, because actually he could only agree with them. Everyone should love her. She was strong, and her belief in him was the strange, unfailing thing. The way that she bonded herself to him, even as he told her about his past, the way that she stood resolute, as he showed her the slums that he'd been born in.

Truly, there seemed to be nothing he could do to lower himself in Astrid's esteem. After a lifetime of finding he could not raise himself in the esteem of others no matter what he did, it was a strange and refreshing thing.

"Is it that simple to undo a lifetime of not loving?" he asked.

"I don't know," Gunnar said. "I personally have yet to overcome much of my life. And I suppose it could be argued that no matter the situation with our parents, that we have had it easier. Astrid certainly had a different situation than I did. An heir and spare cannot, and will not have the same experience. But our parents were hard on her. And if they loved, they did not show it in easy, warm ways. If Astrid loves you, then it is truly an act of bravery. Not just because there has been nothing in our lives to suggest that love is something to aspire to, but because in Astrid's world nothing has been more important than maintaining that facade that she spent her entire life cultivating. That sense of total invulnerability. That sense of perfection. And then she married you. And we all saw those headlines about you. She went with you to Italy, she made a show of being yours no matter what, and I'm not sure that you can possibly understand what that means."

"Because I'm nothing but the son of a whore."

"Because you weren't raised to care quite so much. Your entire world never stopped and turned on your reputation. But for Astrid it did. You don't know what she has given up for you. How could you understand? And yet, she gave you the gift of her love and you threw it back in her face. If you divorce her and humiliate her on top of it…"

"Is that why you're really here? To prevent embarrassment?"

Gunner shrugged a shoulder. "My function in the royal family has never been to prevent embarrassment. Whatever Astrid is, I'm her opposite. My father always felt that I should be the one ruling the country, but I can tell you with great certainty that is not true. She is strong. Not only the strongest woman I know, but the strongest person I have ever had the privilege to be acquainted with. My sister is phenomenal, and you would be privileged to have her. Not because she is blue-blooded. Not because she is a royal, and you're not. But because she has come through our lives with the ability to love, which is more than I can say for myself. The strength in her… If you truly understood it, you would be humbled. But I am not certain that you can. Not unless you find a way to do the same thing she has done."

"I'm tired of receiving lectures from poor little rich kids who imagine that their emotional struggles somehow equal the emotional and physical struggles that I endured. Unless you know what it is to sell your body for a place to stay, I'm not entirely sure we can sit here and compare war wounds."

"Perhaps not," he said. "But then…" He shrugged. "So what?"

"I'm sorry?"

"So what? Your life was hard. Maybe it was harder than mine. Perhaps harder than Astrid's. Perhaps it is a struggle now, for you to figure out how to accept love. But so what?

That part of your life is over now. You have money, you could buy whatever it is you need to make your life whatever it is you want, but the one thing you cannot pay to make better, or make go away, is the situation with my sister. That requires feelings. And it requires work. And in the end, life doesn't care how hard you worked for it. But it might mean more to you. If you figure out the way through. But you won't be given instant happiness simply because it would've been harder for you to sort yourself out than it might be for me."

Gunnar straightened the cuffs on his shirtsleeves, then treated Mauro to the iciest look he'd ever received. "Remember what I said. Do not embarrass my sister. Don't give me a reason to come for you."

And then, as he appeared, Gunnar walked out of his office. Carlo looked around the corner, his expression one of comical concern.

"Leave," Mauro said.

And Carlo vanished instantly.

Mauro was hardly going to listen to the ranting of a rich prince who wouldn't know struggle if it transformed into a snake and bit him in the face. But one thing kept replaying over and over in his head.

So what?

So everything.

Everything.

Because his life had been about struggle. Had been about wanting. And Astrid created more of that feeling inside him than anything else ever had. That ache. That sense of being unsatisfied. Unfulfilled. Of needing more than he would ever be able to have. A desperate hunger that could not be satisfied by food, by money. On that score he was right, as well. Because he knew that this was something that money could not solve. Knew that it was something he would not be able to fix. And that left him feeling...

Helpless. Utterly and completely helpless.

He hated that. There was no depth he would not sink to, he had proved that. He was willing to prostitute himself. He was willing to claw his way up to the top if need be. But there was no clawing here. There were no building towers. There was only...

There was only lowering himself.

As Astrid had said. Making himself into some debased creature all for her, and he didn't have any concept of how he might do that. Of what could possibly entice him to behave in such a way.

To leave all he'd created, to lower all his shields.

To make himself less.

Love.

The need for it, the drive for it… It was the thing that was pushing him forward now. It was the thing that was making him miserable, the thing in his chest that made him want. And he did not understand how he was supposed to do it.

How he was supposed to…

It wasn't fair. She made him ache. She made him feel things, want things, need things that he had sworn he never would again.

Is she the one making you feel this? Or is it you?

And that was when the whole room seemed to turn.

And he wondered.

Perhaps it was Astrid who made him want.

Perhaps it was Astrid who existed to fulfill the want that already existed inside him, and having her there, so close, and not allowing himself to have it all.

Maybe, she was not the problem. Maybe she was the answer to a hole that had already existed. To a need that had been present.

If only he was willing to cross the divide.

If only he was willing to admit that for all his power. For all that he had…

He could not fix it on his own.

He needed her.

He needed her. And he would do whatever he needed to get her back.

"Carlo," he said, his assistant appearing as if by magic. "Ready my plane. We're going back to Bjornland."

"As you wish."

CHAPTER FOURTEEN

ASTRID WAS NOT looking forward to this year's Christmas celebration at all.

It was a massive party, and in her mind, it was a total farce. There was nothing to celebrate. Yes, the impending birth of her son was joyous, but *she* was broken and alone, and it would take some time before she felt anything beyond that.

Still, all had been planned and arranged, and she was expected to participate whether she wanted to or not.

Things at the palace had changed.

In spite of the fact that Mauro was not in residence, her situation with the council was resolved.

While they would still exist, as long as the men wished to hold the office, she would disband it formally once they all retired, or passed on to the next life. And for now they existed as figureheads, symbols, more than anything else.

Which, in her mind, was much better than her existing as such.

The room was full of revelers, crystals dripping from each and every surface of the glorious ballroom.

The Christmas tree loomed large in the corner, a glowing beacon. At least it usually was. Right now the great golden glow mocked her. A symbol of joy and hope when she could feel none of it at all right now.

All of the decorations were ornate, in a way that she didn't truly enjoy, though she'd had her bedroom redone.

The thought made her smile, if somewhat sadly. Because it was something Mauro had said she should do, and even though he had hurt her, she knew that he was right.

And every night she wished that he were there with her.

Even though she shouldn't. Even though she shouldn't wish to see him again. Not ever.

Love, it turned out, did not fade simply because someone wronged you. Love, it turned out, was a terrible inconvenience.

The ball gown she was wearing was a gossamer, floaty confection that hung loosely over her curves, which was a necessity given that they were expanding with each passing day. That was another thing that made her miss him.

He was missing all of the changes, and it made her indescribably sad that this was the case. Guests were being brought forward to where she sat, being presented to her one by one. And there were any number of ushers dressed in navy blue suits, with gold epaulets on their shoulders, traditional dress for noblemen imbuing land.

Astrid was quite bored with it, and trying her best to appear engaged. It wasn't any of her guests' fault that she was brokenhearted, after all.

Out of the corner of her eye, she saw another of the greeters moving toward her, his head bent low. His hands behind his back. He did not have a guest on his arm. She looked at him, and her heart hit the front of her chest.

"What are you…"

"My Queen," he said, bending to one knee in front of her.

Mauro. He was here. And he was dressed as… One of the ushers.

"I had to sneak into your party," he said, his voice low, "especially as my name is mud here at the palace."

"Yes," she said, feeling dizzy. "It is."

"I had to come and find you," he said. "And I took inspiration for how from you. But I have something that I think belongs to you."

He reached out from behind his back, and produced her shoe. That crystalline beauty that she had worn and left behind the night she had seduced him at the club. "I believe this is yours."

"Yes," she said, her throat dry. "It is."

"You would permit me to see, if it fits?"

A bubble of laughter rose up in her throat. "If you must."

"I must," he said gravely. "Because the woman whose foot fits this shoe has something of mine. My heart. But more than that, my everything. I thought… Astrid, I thought that you made me hurt. That you made me incomplete, but that is not true. Instead, you revealed to me the empty space in my soul, and you are the only thing that can fill it. I blamed you, but you are not the problem. You are the solution. And so… Let me see. Do me the honor of showing me if you are in fact the woman who fits the shoe. Who fits that hole inside me."

She slipped her foot out of the shoe she was wearing and held it out to him, not caring that they were drawing stares, that everyone in the room had realized just who he was.

She could see that Gunnar and Latika were barely restraining themselves, allowing her to handle the moment, out of respect for her strength, she knew. But she also knew it was testing them.

She extended her foot to him, and he slipped it on.

A perfect fit.

"My Queen," he said. "I am kneeling before you. I am not in my tower. I am at your feet. And I must humbly confess to you that I love you. But I am a broken man who is nothing more than where I came from. But I love you. I love you, and I will spend all of my days trying to prove to you that I am worthy of that love. For I am nothing without you. I am nothing without this life. And it would not matter if you were a queen, or if we lived back in those slums I worked so hard to escape. Love was the thing that was always missing. And love is the only thing I cannot buy."

"Then it's perfect," she said, sliding out of her throne and dropping to her knees with him. "Because love is the one thing that I cannot legislate. Is the one thing that I cannot bend to my will. I cannot manipulate it, I cannot find an old law that would enable me to capture it and hold it in my hands. Love is all that I need. You are all that I need."

"I love you," he said.

"I love you too."

"You have to stay at this party?"

"It's my party. It's my birthday."

"Happy birthday."

"Thank you," she said, feeling light-headed and surreal, dizzy.

"We have this? Will we have each other forever?" she asked, whispering softly.

"Yes, my Queen. We will have each other, and happily. Ever after."

EPILOGUE

WHEN THE BRAND-NEW Prince of Bjornland came into the world some months later, the media instantly hailed him as perfection. A specimen of humanity that possessed his mother's regal bearing and his father's determination, but no one was half so infatuated with him as his father. And his mother.

"He is perfect," Mauro said decisively, laying him down in the crib that first night, pressing a kiss to his soft, downy head.

"He is," Astrid agreed. "Perfection. As is our life."

"I had thought that happiness was in the top of a high-rise building. Where I had finally overcome. Where I would finally prove to my father that I had value. I climbed up that hill and begged for him to love me, and received nothing in return. Though, I realize now that

I did. I realize now that I learned something I needed right now. Our son will never have to earn my love. And there is nothing he could do to lose it. What our parents did to us… It was never us. It was them. And as for me… Happiness was never alone at the top of a highrise. It is here. With you. With him. Forever."

For the first time in his entire life, Mauro did not feel like a boy from the slums.

Astrid made him a king. Not because of her title, but because she had given him her heart.

And he had given her his.

And that was truly the most powerful thing on earth.

* * * * *

LET'S TALK

Romance

For exclusive extracts, competitions
and special offers, find us online:

f facebook.com/millsandboon

⦿ @millsandboonuk

🐦 @millsandboon

Or get in touch on 0844 844 1351*

For all the latest titles coming soon,
visit millsandboon.co.uk/nextmonth